Anonymous

Wayside Thoughts

SALZWASSER
VERLAG

Anonymous

Wayside Thoughts

Reprint of the original, first published in 1863.

1st Edition 2022 | ISBN: 978-3-37500-351-7

Verlag (Publisher): Salzwasser Verlag GmbH, Zeilweg 44, 60439 Frankfurt, Deutschland
Vertretungsberechtigt (Authorized to represent): E. Roepke, Zeilweg 44, 60439 Frankfurt, Deutschland
Druck (Print): Books on Demand GmbH, In de Tarpen 42, 22848 Norderstedt, Deutschland

WAYSIDE THOUGHTS,

BY

A Christian Pilgrim;

THE RECREATION OF WEARY DAYS.

THE SOLACE OF SUFFERING NIGHTS.

1860—62.

LONDON

1863.

PREFACE.

IF months of almost unremitted suffering bear no fruit for other's good no less than for one's own, its object can scarcely be said to have been attained. How far the attainment in the present case is for the future to decide.

Enough indeed for myself the Record of suffering hours not altogether profitlessly employed, bringing as it does, to the recollection what, I would still believe, were the whisperings of the Spirit the Comforter and the glad Response made to them from within, and still more, enkindling the hope that life yet spared for future duties will be spent, far better than the past, for my Master's glory and the good of my fellow-men. But surely "Consolations abound in order that we may be able to comfort others with the consolation wherewith we are comforted of God." The world of Christian sufferers is large, far greater than can be reached by living tongue; nor are the written pages, wherein the comforted have spoken, yet too numerous for the wide variety of human woe; while the fact will be readily acknowledged, that by far the greater number of volumes intended for its alleviation are repetitions not only of the thoughts, but the words of the speakers. The eye familiar with our written sources of human consolation at once rests, in almost every such volume, upon lines well-known and valued. Nor if a thought of such an honour to be accorded to anything found herein be entertained, let blame attach to me. I would live in the heart of many beyond my own time and generation. I would "though dead, yet speak;" "I have believed and therefore have I spoken;" I know that faith and patience have but to be tried for the very fire to issue in praise. Not mere echoes are to be heard of "voices in the night," but the Pilgrim's songs are to be called forth and felt to harmonize with the notes struck by the great Master-hand. Their language, however simple, shall be recognised as part of the Heavenly Melody, and excite in their fellow-pilgrims their utterance of praise. If mine the privilege of eliciting one such utterance from a fellow-sufferer, I shall know the blessing attained, even though it may be "after many days."

INDEX.

WAYSIDE THOUGHTS.

I.

"And Jesus, going up to Jerusalem, took the twelve disciples apart in the way." Matt. xx. 17.)

TIS not amid the busy throng
  The Christian Pilgrim best is guided,
His steps, though dearest friends among,
  Were never to their care confided;
'Tis not when most engaged in duties,
  How loved soe'er they be and blest,
That man can see the varied beauties
  Which shine upon his way to Rest.

He needs the standing still awhile
  To view the passing landscape o'er,
To measure all the weary toil
  Of his own pathway heretofore,
To value as he ought the pleasures
  So crowded in the toilsome past,
To count the unexhausted treasures
  That still before his feet are cast.

He needs to stand a while aside
  His fellow-Pilgrims to survey,
To watch the restless human tide
  Sweep by him on their headlong way,
To comprehend the unceasing strife
  For things that perish undergone,
To gather truths of death and life
  From circles other than his own.

Perchance he needs some preparation
  For greater calls upon his faith,
And Christ would have his consecration
  Afresh for suffering or death;
In Him to live, by death to gain,
  By teaching this He loves to engage
Our hearts for what may yet remain
  Of our appointed Pilgrimage.

And hence His guidance in the way
  To Zion's earthly temple-court;
He bids His loved disciples stay
  With Him a while, however short;
And then, amid the burning tears
  Such grievous tidings needs must bring,
He pours into their wondering ears
  The future of His suffering.

Their Lord and Master soon must go
  In paths no other feet can tread;
Have they their baptism of woe?
  They shall be ever comforted;
Yet dearest friends must part on earth,
  'Tis what the suffering Lord is teaching,
And joy must draw its very birth
  From faith to Christ ascended reaching.

But oh! their sorrow! Hopes of peace
  All centering in Him for ever,
Well may disciples' courage cease,
  If aught the earthly bond can sever;
Well may they have to stand apart,
  E'en in their happy Zionward way,
To gain fresh strengthening of heart
  For each expected sorrowing day.

Nor less the Christian Pilgrim now
  Is made to seek his strength for toil,
In love he's silenced, or laid low,
  By Jesus bid to rest a while:
But Jesus still remains my guide,
  Nor suffers me to walk alone;
I'll praise then while I stand aside,
  Nor care how long He casts me down.

II.

"Because they have no changes, therefore they fear not God." (Psalm lv. 19.)

When sky above our head is bright,
And not a cloud appears in sight,
'Tis well for us to recollect how soon 'tis overcast,
The storm how suddenly 'tis driven
O'er all the face of brightest heaven,
The days of light and sunshine, oh! how quickly they are past!

Nor less when not a ray of light
Is gilded to our mortal sight,
But all around is thickening in darkness and in storm,
'Tis well to recollect how soon,
Ere earth has reached its very noon,
The clouds all vanish, and again she takes her brightest form.

'Tis thus in mercy God arranges
The constant series of changes,
Whereby the earth exhibits all her wonders to mankind,
The storm, the calm, the sun, the shades,
One loving purpose all pervades,
That man in varied blessings all his happiness shall find.

Were all in sunshine to remain,
And each new day appear again
Clothed as before in summer garb of warmth and joy and brightness,
The heart, so carnal from its birth,
Mid flowers and streams and fields of earth,
Would wander on enchanted and rejoicing in its lightness.

So were unvaried clouds to hang,
Or gather blackness as they rang
With thunder threatening deluges to all the works of man,
The soul would scarce to duty rise,
But, leaving very exercise,
Would pass in idle terror a great portion of life's span.

'Tis change that makes our life appear
A pressing-on from year to year,
To something better than can e'er on this our earth be found;
From infancy to youth, and then
To manhood, and from being men
To old age quickly passing, we are forced to look beyond.

And thus with everything in life;
E'en peace itself is learnt by strife,
Joy has its bitter contrast and is taught us best by sorrow,
Health in its value is unknown
Till sickness with its warnings come;
We only find to-day's true worth by our caring for the morrow.

What then if doubting heart repine
At all the changes that are mine,
Shall not my recollection wake this truth of God's own Word?
Each fearful thought it will reprove,
All fretful faithlessness remove,
"Because there are no changes theirs, they fear not God the Lord."

III.

"Trial no strange thing." (1 Pet. iv. 12.)

WHAT thine inheritance, poor sinful Flesh?
Infirmity, corruption, sickness, death—
Not as thou bearest thy Creator's image,
But as thou sharest thy first parents' fall.

The world a desolation, Nature's taint
O'er all pervading, all Creation groans,
A bright redemption waiting from the Lord.
How shall not then my heart cease wondering
At daily trials or at hourly toils?
My labours in the vineyard stopped awhile,
The tongue forbidden to speak, the heart to plead,
My flock deserted, and a foreign home,
The fondest hopes just in their budding nipped,
What but a proper expectation this
If rightly weighing my infirmities?—
'Tis health that I am seeking, sickness comes,
The aid of the physician sought in vain,
Nor yet the Great Deliverer unasked
To bless the skill of man—the body fails
Yet more and more; the very breath of life
Seems shortened and is rendered difficult;
The days of suffering lengthened, and the nights
Denied their wonted respite from the toil;
What less shall a poor sinful man expect,
Who knows his frailty and who asks for good?—
The mind, bright emanation from on high
But clogged with earthly teachings and obscured,
Shall this escape the chastening? Why, it shares
Each feebleness of body and each toil:
'Twere strange if its best power did not fail,
And in its turn the minister become

To yet more feebleness. The Soul, though saved
From the eternal sin-wrought punishment,
Is yet confined within the fleshly bond,
Shall darkness then be stranger to its path?
Thou hast not learned thy being yet aright,
O man, that dost of punishment complain,
Thy nature and its need, its source, its light,
Its end, unfitness, and yet hope of Heaven—
And hast thou not forgotten to compare
Thine own with others' sufferings? How few
Thy trials are, and theirs so numberless!
Alone how many weep! Thy grief is shared—
Unaided many a sufferer, thou art nursed
And cherished with the tenderest of care—
With blessings compassed, they deprived of all—
No love their brightness, smiles are all for thee—
'Tis strange that others nearer Heaven by far
Should less be blessed, and thou so comforted!—
But stranger far that thou should'st e'er forget
The Chief of Sufferers, the Anointed One,
Born in the stable yet the Lord of lords,
A child obedient yet of all the King,
By man despised yet living to caress,
Of every woe the Sharer, for He bore
The whole world's sorrows when He bore its sins.
The Guiltless Sufferer, no taint nor share
Of sin was His and yet its Thorns He wore.

Then think of Jesus and be comforted—
Yea, humbled soul, that knowest thy desert,
The heritage of sin, and sorrow's curse,
That lookest for the chastisement from Heaven
As well deserved and bearing its intent,
Oh! think of Jesus and be comforted—
How low soe'er our nature, He can raise
The lowest to Redemption's pinnacle;
Already hath He sanctified a part
By taking it Himself before the Throne;
And thy shortcomings, feebleness, and sin,
All, all shall be forgotten by the Lord
Who smites in mercy and corrects in love.
Mind, body, soul, whate'er to thee belongs
Is under His direction, and He knows
When best to chasten and how best to raise.
Be sure of this, His Love, His Care are thine,
He truly suffered, and for thee He died.

IV.

"O spare me, that I may recover strength, before I go hence, and be no more." (Psalm xxxix. 13.)

FAIN would I linger yet
  Before my summons come,
Things of the past forget
  While pressing for my home.

Spare me, O Saviour, spare,
  Nor bid me to Thy side;
Earth has for me its care,
  For which I would abide.

My strength has failed me now
  So rapidly and long,
I scarce remember how
  To sing the Pilgrim's song.

There is so much undone
  Of what I have to do,
Were it for this alone
  I hesitate to go.

My labours incomplete,
  My lips Heaven's song untaught,
I know not how to meet
  The Judge of every thought.

For self, for others too,
  There is so much I need;
Saviour, I cannot go,
  Thy sparing Love I plead.

Spare me, O Saviour, spare,
  Yet not for suffering,
But to enjoy my share
  Of happy labouring.

My former strength I ask,
  Yea, Thine wrought out in me,
That I my appointed task
  May work right faithfully.

And when by Grace 'tis ended,
  Then bid me, Lord, to come,
My work with Thine well-blended,
  Perfect will be my Home.

V.

"Now we see through a glass, darkly; but then face to face." (1 Cor. xiii. 12.)

WHAT know we here below,
Poor Creatures of a Day?
Unknown each step we go
Along our weary way:
Dark, through a glass, our brightest vision here,
For Power Divine nigh fails to make it clear.

Dost wonder that the cloud
So often intervenes?
Or darkness should enshroud
Life's purest, happiest scenes?
'Tis that our aching vision should be spared,
And thus for future usefulness prepared.

Yet, oh! how longs the Mind
To pierce the very sky!
To wander unconfined
O'er its futurity!
But Mercy 'tis the unforeseen conceals,
Nor to the longing heart its paths reveals.

Dark then let vision be;
  Enough is fully known,
Hereafter shall we see
  Our path with flowers strown;
E'en blindness-self a real blessing prove,
And bounded sight a gift of Perfect Love.

Be sure that what is ours
  Is happiest and best;
Our noblest, highest powers
  Need curbing, peace, and rest;
Could clearest faith the present life survey,
How deep our longings to be far away!

Or were its pathway traced
  In characters of joy,
Its labours all embraced
  In holiest employ,
How should we cling to this our sin-stained earth,
Or value life beyond its proper worth!

Praise then be ours to give
  For this our bounded sight,
'Twere not for man to live
  In an unclouded light;
The cloud, the darkness, and the twilight here
Are blessed tokens of a happier sphere.

Nor long shall sight be dim;
  Christ has prepared a place
Where we shall rest in Him,
  And see Him face to face;
That will be vision boundless and complete
When all perfections in the Lord shall meet.

Lord, make it mine, I pray,
  Let faith embrace the hour
When shadows flee away
  Before Thy rising power;
Content I'll wait, and patient learn to trace,
Each gleam of brightness from Thy wondrous grace.

VI.

"As thy days, so shall thy strength be." (Deut. xxxiii. 25.)

Life's morning, as the sunlight warms it, shines;
Life's evening sets because its sun declines;
Its midday glories on its Lord depend,
From Him its birth, continuance, and end.

And yet what hindrances the spirit chill
Ere life's acknowledged purpose we fulfil!
Its best desire, its most exalted aim,
Do but its earthly origin proclaim.

Renewed and chastened, purified by fire,
Its upward flight would fain be daily higher,
Yet see how each reiterated blow
Curtails its power, or even lays it low.

How needed then some Promise to sustain!
Whence power sufficient to support it gain?
The answer clear; we find it in the Word,
The Promise sure, for strength is in the Lord.

"E'en as thy days, so shall His strength be Thine,"
Thy strength from Him, 'tis sure because divine;
Thy power according to thy need is lent,
And grace sufficient for each duty sent.

Long, weary, sin-tried is thy pilgrimage?
The longer dost thou Heavenly aid engage.
Brief and uncertain, hastening to decay,
Are these thy days? more aided is thy way.

Thy days are clouded and their light obscured,
Thy footsteps through the wilderness allured?
The nearer is the Arm on which to rest,
Thyself of God more lovingly caressed.

The dearest ties of earth are seen to break,
And one by one the hand of death to take?

The Heavenly Presence is the closer brought,
And power to grasp it the more surely taught.

Dost ask what truth thou should'st from this receive?
Thine all to an Almighty Father leave:
Thy days appointed, guarded in His hand,
Life, death, and glory are at His command.

VII.

"Peace, be still." (Mark iv. 39.)

"PEACE, be still," rebellious spirit,
  Child of an apostate race;
Would'st thou wrath as well inherit,
  Loss of all protecting grace?

"Peace, be still," what can rejection
  Of th' Almighty's will avail?
Can it alter the complexion
  Of one loss thy sins entail?

"Peace, be still:" it is the teaching
  Of a love that knows thy want—
Love that to the future reaching,
  Would thy waywardness supplant.

"Peace, be still:" He calms the tossing
  Of the most tempestuous sea;
Thinkest thou, thy will in crossing,
  His power bears no calm to thee?

"Peace, be still:" there is a reason
  For each storm He wills to send;
Doubt a trouble,—it is treason,
  If thou knowest not its end.

"Peace, be still:" of Satan's error
  Thy rebellion thus partakes;
Wonder not if home of terror
  Thine own headstrong folly makes.

"Peace, be still:" 'tis Heaven's treasure
  After a long toil enjoyed;
Let it be thy choicest pleasure
  In its search to be employed.

"Peace, be still:" yet none save Jesus
Can the rebel spirit break;
But He died, He lives to free us
For His Name's, His Glory's sake.

"Peace, be still:" 'tis He must bid it;
He must chain and guide the will:
By a word He calms the spirit,
And He speaks it, "Peace, be still."

VIII.

"The day is thine, the night also is thine: thou hast prepared the light and the sun." (Psalm lxxiv. 16.)

THE day is Thine, O Lord, and Thine the night;
Who dares to question Thine unerring hand?
Thou hast the sun prepared, and formed the light;
Who doubts obedience to Thy just command?

My rebel heart would gladly find excuse
For some rejection of Thy gracious will;
In health, so easy is it to refuse,
So hard in suffering-hour to lie still!

Then bless'd the Spirit that imprints Thy word
  Upon the very portals of my heart;
That makes both health and sickness to record
  How great, how merciful, O Lord, Thou art.

Thine is the day, I have rejoiced to learn,
  From Thee my strength, from Thee to serve the hour;
No word to speak, no step is mine to turn,
  But Thou in love apportionest the power.

Thine is the night, at length I have been taught
  To feel its darkness as a gift from Thee;
By Thee each step of sorrow has been brought,
  That I in all may know Thy constancy.

And Thine I would have day and night to be,
  Safe in Thy hands as long as life shall last;
Their joys and sorrows I'll derive from Thee,
  Till shade and sunshine are for ever past.

IX.

"Be of good cheer; it is I; be not afraid." (Matt. xiv. 27.)

STORM-TOSSED, and toiling Masterless,
The best loved servants of the Lord may be;
Cast down, despairing, powerless,
Feeling full sadly their infirmity:
Behold the loved disciples thus in perilous distress
Toiling by their Lord's command upon the Sea of Galilee.

Not Masterless then, sufferer,
Although thy path be on the stormy sea;
Appointed by the Saviour,
That path is one wherein you ought to be:
Be sure 'tis prayer-defended by the Great Deliverer,
No less than were disciples on the Sea of Galilee.

Long dreary hours of toil were theirs;
And dost thou think there shall be less for thee?
Nor, when the Lord Himself appears,
The form of loving Master can they see:
Ah! wonder not that Jesus' presence should excite thy fears;
'Twas thus with the disciples on the Sea of Galilee.

He walked upon the highest waves—
No crest too high, no blast of storm too free;
O'er all, in all, from all He saves—
His power boundless as Eternity:
He plucks as He sees fit, from earthly tomb or ocean graves;
'Twas thus He saved His servants on the Sea of Galilee.

Their souls within them terrified,
'Tis e'en a spirit that they think they see;
Nor scarce less fearful when He cried,
"Be of good cheer, why thus affrighted be?
'Tis I; be not afraid; your loving Master at your side,
What evil can befall you on the Sea of Galilee?"

O Gracious Voice of Love Divine!
Soft with the words of tender sympathy!
How oft, when scarce I knew them Thine,
Hast Thou in loving-kindness beamed on me!
Well may I take Thy cheering words, and ever make them mine,
They comforted disciples on the Sea of Galilee.

When earthly trials overwhelm,
And storms of dreaded ill encompass me;
When tempests o'er me hurrying seem,
And troubles gather in intensity,
I'll think of One, not only near, but guiding at the helm,—
The same that cheered His servants on the Sea of Galilee.

"Be of good cheer, thou troubled heart,"
Engraven on each darkest cloud I see;
"'Tis I, and I would bear a part
In all thy complicated misery."
Thus would I hear the Voice of Love at troubles' each new smart—
The Voice that spoke with power on the Sea of Galilee.

"Be not afraid;" and stilled is fear,
No more shall strengthened heart urge terror's plea:
Nay, if He bids me to draw near
On highest waters of the troubled sea,
I shrink not at the summons, for I've simply learned to hear
The Voice that spoke Divinely on the Sea of Galilee.

X.

"There remaineth a rest to the people of God." (Heb. iv. 9.)

I KNOW there's a rest by the light of creation,
'Twas the dawn of the future when the world was complete,
'Twas the Saviour's blest Sabbath that knows no cessation,
The centre of glory where His attributes meet.

I know there's a rest by the Paradise blessings
In the time of man's innocence fully enjoyed;
As for Man, he was born for paternal caressings,
And in Sabbath communion is he fitly employed.

I know there's a rest by the glow yet remaining
From the Sun which then rose to give light to our race,
Nor has Sin's darkened landscape, its features retaining,
Prevailed the glad rays of that light to efface.

I know there's a rest by the absence of Jesus;
Where'er He is present in glory there's peace;
I can feel that in mercy He's preparing to free us,
And His work when accomplished is perfect release.

I know there's a rest by the wants of the toiling,
By the streams so abundant of sorrowers' tears,
By the storms of affliction the purest hearts soiling,
By the cries of the mourner, by the sinking one's fears.

I know there's a rest by the thirst of the spirit—
Every beat of its pulse is a proof of its home;
There are joys in the future that it longs to inherit,
And its cravings are met by the rest yet to come.

I know there's a rest by the promise once made me;
'Tis the rest of the angels no less than my own;
'Tis the rest of my Father, and the Spirit has bade me
Look to Him for my hope of enjoyment alone.

I know there's a rest by the joys that enliven,
By the conquests I'm gaining and the struggles sustained;
How the tongue will rejoice when the blessing is given
To be telling for ever how the rest was obtained!

XI.

"Wherefore doth a living man complain, a man for the punishment of his sins?" (Lam. iii. 39.)

AND wherefore doth a man,
A living man, complain
  Of that which God apportions
    Of trial's time or place?
His mind on folly set,
He surely must forget
  The thousand solemn cautions
    Of reason and of grace.

The Lord of our salvation,
On whom each distant nation
  Shall ere long suppliant call,
    The Lord of love and might,
The Lord of earth and heaven,
To whom all power is given,
  Shall not He, the Judge of all,
    Do only what is right?

Then measure what is sent
As 'twere in punishment,
  What trial can be greater than
    A man's desert of sin?

Let every blessing cease;
Let there be no release
From trouble, even then man's
Complaint should ne'er begin.

What if the soul be tossed,
And purposes be crossed,
And all seems made to minister
To sorrow's sharpest blow?
The soul is not so free
As it was wont to be,
And purposes full sinister
Have stopped the spirit's flow.

Have riches taken wing?
Do sad reverses bring
A loss of the position
So covetéd by all?
Some failure there must be
Of heart's simplicity,
So painful the transition,
So terrible the fall!

What if the body fail,
And sicknesses entail
The loss of all the power
The frame has long enjoyed?

Has there been no abuse,
Without one true excuse,
  Of every passing hour
    That could be well employed?

The eyes, oh! how they wander!
The hands, oh! how they pander
  To the heart's too ready seeking
    Some strange forbidden fruit!
The lips of guile so full,
So indolent the soul,
  The tongue e'en shrinks from speaking
    Before the throne its suit.

No wonder if in wrath
The Lord should hedge our path,
  And silence every utterance
    From creatures so defiled;
For let us not forget
That 'tis in mercy yet
  Existence is a sufferance
    From punishment beguiled.

Grant then the trial sent
By way of punishment,—
  Its object judgment, not in love
    A sinner's heart to win;

Still would we say again,
Shall living man complain
At trials sent to prove
The height, the depth, of sin?

The rather should we wonder
That Sinai's loud thunder
Has not proclaimed in anger
The sinner's awful doom;
He lives, and life is spared
That Jesus may be heard
Delivering from danger
And rifling the tomb.

We live: then ne'er again
Will coward heart complain
Of trial's fiercest hour
Encompassing the soul;
We look to Jesus' cross,
And count all else but loss,
That we may gain the power
For fear's, for faith's control.

XII.

FEAR'S MURMURINGS AND FAITH'S ANSWERS.

FEAR'S MURMURINGS.

WHEN days are dark and dreary,
And earth itself is cold,
The heart grows sad and weary,
Cast in a kindred mould;
When corn invites no reaping,
And harvest is delayed,
The Pastor thinks with weeping
Of souls that are half dead.

FAITH'S ANSWER.

And what though the vines be failing,
Or the fig-tree no blossom bear?
Not a cry shall be heard of wailing,
Not a thought be embraced of fear:
My heart shall its courage gather
From the Lord who protects His own,
I know that my Heavenly Father
Never leaves His own work undone.

FEAR'S MURMURINGS.

The storm around us darkens,
  The sky is overcast,
Each ear with terror hearkens
  To showers falling fast:
Fit emblem, thinks the Pastor,
  Of dangers to his home,
From Satan working faster
  Because his hour is come.

FAITH'S ANSWER.

And what though the Lord should tarry,
  Or His chariot stay its course?
Not a promise of His can miscarry,
  Not a word ever lose its force;
For the time of distress and sorrow
  He has promised His special grace;
In His hand is the unknown morrow,
  And each lamb has its chosen place.

FEAR'S MURMURINGS.

But see what changes hasten!
  What troubles without end!
How Death's sharp talons fasten
  On dearest, strongest friend!

Whose welcome kind shall gladden
The Pastor's late return?
Whose loss his heart shall sadden?
Who cease with love to burn?

FAITH'S ANSWER.

What though the earth be upheaving,
And the hills be o'erwhelmed by the sea?
Not a fear shall disturb my believing
That the Lord is a Father to me:
And, if Father, I know He's providing
Each blessing and mercy enjoyed,
But I think not of one as abiding,
Or the gold to be mine unalloyed.

FEAR'S MURMURINGS.

What too if sickness lingers,
And trials new unfold?
Perchance Death's icy fingers
On me may lay their hold:
What if no friendly greeting
Shall e'er again be given?
Or tongue should cease repeating
The claims and joys of Heaven?

FAITH'S ANSWER.

E'en though the Lord should slay me,
 Yet in Him will I put my trust;
Not a power of Death shall delay me,
 Though the flesh be returned to its dust:
Nought from Jesus and Heaven can sever
 The dear ones surrounding Him there,
We shall meet, as redeemèd for ever,
 Eternity's glory to share.

XIII.

"It pleased the Father that in Him (Christ Jesus) should all fulness dwell." (Col. i. 19.)

In sorrow's chill hour when in vain aid is sought,
When the soul to the verge of despair has been brought,
How full of sweet comfort and blessing the thought,
 Jesus is mine!

By Satan assaulted, how deep the dejection
Of heart and of soul from the sad recollection
Of failures so frequent! Then blest the reflection,
 Jesus knows all!

The sins of the past rise in judgment to frighten,
While the mercies neglected th' ingratitude heighten,
A single remembrance all my hope seems to brighten,
Jesus is Saviour.

The path of the future is beset all around
With dangers unnumbered, and terrors abound,
What joy should be ours one truth to have found,
Jesus yet lives.

For what as to darkness when the true light is given?
Who speaks of despair when supported from Heaven?
By one revelation from the soul fear is driven,
Jesus is all.

Let Satan assault us with trouble or wo,
With fiercer temptations and heaviest blow,
We ne'er can forget he's a well-vanquished foe,
Jesus has conquered.

Let conscience accuse us of sin and transgression,
So deep and continued as to baffle confession,
Full pardon we find in the one blest expression,
Jesus has died.

And so for the future, our Jesus yet lives,
And grace and support in abundance He gives,
Each saint hope and joy from the blessing derives,
Jesus is King.

Then courage, faint-hearted, be cast down no longer
If Satan be strong, there is One who is stronger,
'Tis Jesus, King, Saviour, the Victor though Crucified,
He knows all, He is all, He lives though He died,
And Jesus is Thine.

XIV.

THE TEACHER AND THE TAUGHT.

"For our light affliction, which is but for a moment, worketh for us a far more exceeding and eternal weight of glory." (2 Cor. iv. 17.)

WHO shall now speak of his afflictions' weight?
The burthen who shall now refuse to bear?
If thus th' Apostle calls his sufferings light
And finds so much his weary heart to cheer?

On every side in trouble, yet his mind
Free from distress: perplexed his soul within,
Yet not despairing; privileged to find,
Though persecuted, sympathy Divine.

Cast down in heart, yet rising from the blow;
And bearing in his body Jesus' death,
E'en thus he faints not, for though lying low
He lives to Christ the more by every breath.

And hence he calls his deep afflictions light;
  They last but for a moment, and are charged
With greater and eternal glory's weight,
  Their subject strengthened and their scope enlarged.

THE TAUGHT.

Light my trials and temptation,
  When with others they're compared:
Oh! for greater resignation
  From the knowing they are shared!

Shared by Saints, Apostles, Martyrs,
  Heroes of the written Word;
Shared by Adam's sons and daughters,
  Feeblest servants of the Lord.

Light my trials when I measure
  The desert of life-long sin;
Light when thinking of the treasure
  That improved they bear within.

"For a moment" is my sorrow,
  Should it last a whole life's span,
Joy is sure to come to-morrow,
  So does Mercy deal with man.

Nay, my trials are a blessing
  In the work they have to do,
Standing out a plain confessing
  Of a glory now in view.

Their aim to fix the soul on Heaven,
  And for glory to prepare,
With Christ to suffer it is given,
  And His kingdom thence to share.

What shall I then call my trials?
  Pledges of the promised land,
Not of wrath, but peace, the vials,
  Poured from Jesus' loving hand.

Shall I bear them? Yea, I'll praise Him,
  Glorious giver of all joy,
Seek in all my woes to trace Him,
  And rejoice in the employ.

XV.

PRECIOUS PROMISES.

"When thou passest through the waters, I will be with thee; and through the rivers, they shall not overflow thee: when thou walkest through the fire, thou shalt not be burned." (Isaiah xliii. 2.)

SORROWING brother, cease to listen
To the torrents' deaf'ning sound,
See the *waters* sunlit glisten,
Though the clouds are gath'ring round.

Suffering brother, leave, I pray you,
Shudd'ring at the depth of *river*,
See the Guide who'll ne'er betray you,
Standing ready to deliver.

Sin-scarred brother, wait no longer
Testing what the heat of *fire*,
The flame of Heavenly Love is stronger,
See its light is spreading higher.

'Twere enough for sinful creatures,
Living in a world of wo,
To be sure that sorrow's features
Must be scanned by all below:

Yet it bears a higher teaching,
Hear its words of tender love,
Human wo is ever reaching
To a Brother's heart above:

And that Brother bids us call Him
"Dear companion, tenderest guide,"
Thus for all that can befall him
Man shall feel a friend beside.

Oh! how clear His voice entreating
Ere a drop of sorrow falls,
Words of comfort oft repeating
How to fearful souls He calls!

"When thou goest through the *waters*
I am with thee, sorrowing friend,
Tell it to thy sons and daughters,
Heavenly patience knows no end:

"When thou goest through the *river*
Not a ripple shall o'erflow thee,
I am with thee to deliver,
Surest hand is then below thee.

"When thou walkest through the *fires*
  Fear no roar of kindling flame,
Love's no feeblest spark expires,
  Ever is its light the same."

Say we then, O brother, truly
  That the streams are glistening bright,
Warn we every sorrower duly
  Lest he dread the river's height:

What of fire or torrent's roaring?
  Voice there is above all wo,
Drawn by that allurement, soaring
  Souls may lose all sounds below.

XVI.

"Watchman, what of the night? Watchman, what of the night? The watchman said, The morning cometh, and also the night." (Isaiah xxi. 11, 12.)

WHAT of the night? Watchman, say,
    What of the night?
Though sun be far away
    The moon is bright;
What of the night? Watchman, what dost thou say?
Thou hast seen all of it: tell me, I pray.

"The morning is coming fast,
"So is the night;
"The hours they hurry past,
"Soon 'twill be light,
"The day comes, the night comes." So doth the Watchman say;
Heed it, ye sleepers, drive your slumbers away.

'Tis in night that the sleeper wakes,
Darkness around;
When for soul a man counsel takes,
Trials abound;
Blessed be the word then of Watchman, we say,
For it tells more of night than it does of the day.

Do the nights become drearier,
Sorely-tried soul?
And the heart it grows wearier,
Beyond controul?
The night may be dark, yet drive sorrow away,
Thy fears shall the sunlight of morning allay.

Nor is it all dark around,
Moon shineth clear;
Some help, if not light, is found,
Watchman is here:
Are the night-watches ours? Bid them welcome we may,
For they teach us to watch, and to wait, and to pray.

Night and day may be dreariest,
Oh, who can tell?
When the tried are the weariest,
Know it is well:
And think it not wisdom in sorrow to say,
"How I dread the long night, how I long for the day!"

Leave to God times of sorrow, friend,
All is not night;
If we must seek a morrow's end,
Look for the light:
One moment desire and long for we may,
'Tis the dawn of the morning, eternity's day.

The day of my Master Lord,
And it is mine:
I have his undoubted word,
He there doth shine;
Our sorrows all ended, our tears wiped away,
Oh! for the foretaste of that cloudless day!

XVII.

"For we know that if our earthly house of this tabernacle were dissolved, we have a building of God, an house not made with hands, eternal in the heavens." (2 Cor. v. 1.)

AND is this mortal frame
For dissolution made?
Shall men of boundless fame
Within the earth be laid?
A temple of the Everliving God
Be mixed with earth, an undistinguished clod?

Poor tenement of clay,
How frail thy lifelong power!
The creature of a day!
The sport of every hour!
Thy helpless ruin from thy birth begun,
Though years from time's inheritance be won.

Who shall not mourn thy fall?
Thy frailty who forget?
For give to joy thy all,
Thou art but dust as yet,
Thy brightest days a period of decay,
Thy highest beauties doomed to pass away.

Yet art thou image bright
  Of God, though under curse,
Reflexion of the light
  That warms the universe,
And hence immortal, though of worms the heir,
In endless glory destined to appear.

Peace to thy very dust!
  We hail its destiny;
When death's strong chain is burst,
  Thy triumph we shall see,
Each grain of thine bears germ of life within,
Thou losest earth, eternity to win.

Oh! for the glorious change
  For this our frame prepared!
How all its powers will range
  O'er realms by angels shared!
The Master calls, the dead in Christ obey,
And forms celestial rise to endless day.

Awake, O dust, awake,
  The Master He is nigh;
Prepare thy place to take
  With Him above the sky;
Like Him appear, and see Him as He is
Surrounded by His Heavenly companies.

Thy form no more arrayed
In perishable clay,
Thy purest gold displayed,
Thy dross all purged away:
The perfect temple shall for ever shine
With light and glory that in Christ are thine.

XVIII.

DEATH—TO THE EYE OF SENSE.

WHAT is death? Go, ask the *Monarch*
Seated on the proudest throne,
Power beyond him, stern and dark,
King of Terrors he will own.

What is death? Go, ask the *mother*
Of her infant just bereft,
She tells in grief she cannot smother
Of a cruel act of theft.

What is death? Go, hear the *moaning*
Of the Victor's battlefields,
Mid triumphs conscience must be owning
Conquests that the tyrant wields.

What is death? Behold the *deluge*
Sweeping past in pestilence,
Not a hope is found of refuge,
Human skill is impotence.

What is death? Behold the *nations*
Perishing from age to age,
Endless stream without cessation,
Close of every pilgrimage.

Ruthless tyrant, at thy power
Well may boldest stand appalled,
Naught avails thy hand to lower,
King of Terrors rightly called.

Such is death to mortal senses,
Foe unknown though ever near,
Scatt'ring all our vain pretences,
Every step a cause of fear.

Sin its parent, sin its token,
Sin its never-failing sting,
Well may soul of man be broken
In the hand of such a King.

Well may every hope within me
  Sink at its uncurbed approach;
What can to a smile then win me,
  E'en its presence my reproach?

Seen by eye of sense it makes me
  In each pulse with dread to thrill,
Courage fails, and hope forsakes me,
  Taken captive at its will.

XIX.

DEATH—TO THE EYE OF FAITH.

WERE eye of sense alone to guide us
  Who could bear on earth to live?
Well knowing what must soon betide us
  E'en to death our all to give?

But 'tis not so the Lord has bound us
  To the body of this death,
His loving Providence has found us
  Blest release in eye of faith.

And this Heaven-sent sure director
Not mere things of earth reveals,
But it claims to be protector,
Breaking of the grave the seals:

Faith our guide, nor less defender,
Strips of every fear the tomb,
Opening to our view the splendour
Of the eternal living home.

What is our death? If heart be asking,
Answer is at once prepared,
No need of fear's or fancy's tasking,
'Tis a step by Jesus shared.

Shared by Him the Lord of Glory,
Oh how changed its every feature!
'Tis ours, not death's, the victory,
Ransomed from its power the creature:

Ransomed and victorious proving,
What shall make our hearts afraid?
Sting and burthen once removing
Jesus on Himself hath laid.

What then death to heirs of Heaven?
Gilded portal to the Mansion
Which to Sons of God is given,
Opening of life's expansion!

What is death? The *glorious passage*
To a bright inheritance;
Cold and cheerless? Yet the *presage*
Of the soul's assured advance.

What is death? As *Jordan's river*
Stream by Jesus' presence blest,
Waters opened to deliver
Sons when journeying to rest.

What is death? A *peaceful sleeping*
Of the body we now have:
Cause of nature's saddest weeping
When it views the loved one's grave;

Yet how soul of friend rejoices
When the glorious scenes unfold,
Where the lost ones mingle voices
With the angels' harps of gold!

Death may be the bitter breaking
  Of the dearest human ties,
But no less is it the *waking*
  Of celestial harmonies.

Where thy sting then, tyrant dreaded?
  Where thy victory, O grave?
Jesus by His death has pleaded,
  Jesus living loves to save.

And faith tells me, when I'm treading
  In the valley of death's shade,
That the Lord for me is pleading,
  Willing, waiting, pledged to aid.

Shall I e'er henceforth be fearing
  As I journey to the tomb?
Peace, my soul, as thou art nearing
  Thine own blest eternal home.

Wake, O wake, thou living power,
  Precious gift of simple faith,
Anticipate the coming hour
  Of the mortal body's death.

Give thy flight its full expansion,
Rise with an untiring wing,
Death's a welcome to the mansion
Of the everliving King.

XX.

Nice, Sept. 12, 1860.—The Emperor of the French pays his first visit to his newly acquired dominions.

HAIL! self-created monarch of as fair a land
As e'er was taught to bow to emperor's command!
Thy people greet thee as their own appointed lord,
Yet mid their shouts of welcome hear a stranger's word:
Would that to thee to learn this solemn truth were given,
That none but righteous thrones are owned and blessed of Heav'n.

What though to thee, Oh King, belongs a magic name
To France recalling memories of her proudest fame,
To thee suggestive of the empire of the world,
And kings from ancient thrones by imperial vict'ries hurled?
Forget not Him to whom the proudest must succumb,
The Victor's double exile, and his desert tomb.

Wouldst thou, as though obedient to his thirst for gain,
Extend thy fair dominion to the Rhenish plain?
Thy claim scarce yet established to the Alpine height,
Wouldst thou secure the Rhine by treaty or by fight?
Midst all thy conquests let this simple truth be told,
A nation's subject heart can ne'er be forced nor sold.

Or should perchance a subtle thought be entertained
Of that which ne'er in highest glory could be gained,
Proud Albion's fall? and dost thou plan to wipe away
The stain of Waterloo, that marks thy name for ay?
A million warrior voices seem to rend the air,
"Know that thou hast to beard the Lion in his lair!"

"The empire it is peace," thine own deliberate word,
Let then its peaceful echoes every day be heard;
Disband thy forces gathered at thy stern command,
At best to prey upon the vitals of thy land;
Know that thy truest glory is to check their rage,
And in the arts of peace their highest powers engage.

France has unsullied glories in the empire past,
Borne down to ages e'en as long as time shall last;
Thou canst add naught in war to her imperial fame,
The world acknowledges her widest martial claim;
Thy destiny is peace, and to enhance her might
As arbitress of nations' wrong and freedom's right.

And wilt thou not accept the honour which is given,
A world-wide power of good appointed thee of Heaven?
Lay bare thine arm, if lust of war constrain,
And deluge Europe's fairest plains with blood again,
But know, whatever power or might thou dost employ,
There is a King above, almighty to destroy.

By Him kings reign on earth and monarchs hold
their throne,
He has the nations in His hand and He alone;
Obey his righteous laws, thy throne shall ne'er be
moved,
France guided by his counsel, and thy cause approved,
Crowns of eternal glory shall be given to thee,
And bless'd of Heaven and earth shall be thy dynasty.

XXI.

THOUGHTS SUGGESTED BY PSALM LXXXIV.

"The prisoner of the Lord kept from the sanctuary."

WHAT these bands their glad way bending,
Day by day their line extending,
To Zion, city of their King?
Heart and tongue so well employing,
Surely they have cause for joying,
Thus constrained it is they sing.

Yes, glad pilgrims, well may voices
Tell that every heart rejoices,
  Strange if chorus did not swell;
Ye are of salvation speaking,
While its temple ye are seeking,
  And ye know its portals well.

Thrice the glad assembly calls you,
Year by year no chance befalls you
  As you wend your well-known way,
Blessed feast, that well supplieth
Every want that in you lieth,
  Whose glad step would e'er delay?

None can fail when God is guiding;
On His perfect love confiding,
  Sure ye go from strength to strength;
Where no streams abundance proffer,
Spring or well pure waters offer,
  And all reach your home at length.

And when shall I my steps be bending,
Gratitude its quickness lending,
  To the courts of worship here?
Month by month my day-cloud thickens
This poor dying body sickens,
  Chilling hope and kindling fear.

Sabbath after Sabbath passes,
Blessed tokens in life's mazes
  Of its end and purpose now,
Yet for me no congregation,
No, nor solemn invitation
  Doth the Lord to me allow.

Lord, in such a time of trial,
Time of privilege-denial,
  What can thy poor servant do?
Seek a Spring that's never failing,
Try a Source for ay availing,
  Cast himself on Thee alone.

Lord of Love, then let Thy favour
Beam on me, and thus the savour
  Of Thy House with me shall dwell;
Father, do Thou Thyself become
My Sanctuary and my Home,
  I shall then Thy way know well.

How Thou dost in Love deny me
Temple service, e'en to try me,
  If in Christ I find my joy;
If, when earthly blessings fail me
And no prayers of hope avail me,
  I can still glad praise employ.

Yes, and, as the weeks are flying,
I am with Thy will complying,
  Learning as to things of earth,
How they perish in the using,
Without man's the least abusing,
  At the best, but little worth.

Things of Heaven, these I'm learning
How beyond the earth, discerning
  Whence their real source and spring;
Let me only this be reaching,
Hard though be the mode of teaching,
  And true worship I shall bring.

So when Thou hast fully taught me
All through Christ is daily brought me,
  He the channel and the fount,
Other waters, I'll reject them,
Purest waters, I'll expect them,
  From the real Zion-Mount.

Only be Thou very nigh me,
With Thy strength and grace supply me,
  I will learn to bear Thy will;
Content to find a power reach me
That is willing thus to teach me
  Faith's first precious truth, "Be still."

XXII.

"Jesus wept." (John xi. 35.)

"Jesus wept":—behold the man
Is one with us in sorrowing, no less than one in joy:
Love refuse Him, if we can,
Or in His blessed company a chastened heart t'employ.

"Jesus wept":—a grave the scene,
And friendly eyes were near Him there, all moistened with their tears;
Oh! if near Him I had been,
I could not better love the Lord, or banish all my fears.

"Jesus wept":—then fears of death,
Fears of the sad parting with the friends of loving days,
All are hushed, and every breath
Of doubting is now silenced as to God's appointed ways.

"Jesus wept":—by act divine
He sanctified our suffering, and made it holy ground:
What if sorrow then be mine?
My soul shall e'er rejoice in this, His footsteps to have found.

"Jesus wept":—let every wo
Find its own glad refuge in our Rock's unfailing shade,
Making of each step we go
A path of consecration wherein Jesus lends His aid.

XXIII.

THE PASTOR'S DOUBLE HARVEST.

"They that sow in tears shall reap in joy." (Psalm cxxvi. 5.)

There is no fallow-time for thee, my soul;
If such there can be, it must surely be
When sowing most for others, toiling hard
To break unwilling soil, and planting deep
In that bright vineyard plot marked out for thee.
And so it has been: for in keeping it
Thine own poor garden-ground thou hast not kept:
'Twas lying far too fallow;—hence the love,
That blesses labourer and labour too,

Has bade thee leave thy plot awhile, and see
The power that fits for the successful toil.
In tears must be thy sowing—thou shalt learn
To weep for all thy feebleness, fatigue,
And fickleness of service, thine unrest
When peace was ordered, and thy fears when faith,
The souls ungained, the brands from fire unplucked
The poor unaided, and the babes unfed,
Thy Gospel's sad uncertainty of sound,
A Father's love untaught or unexplained,
A Saviour's fulness limited, the work
Of full free grace unfelt if not unsought;
For these thou hast to weep, and weeping learn
How best to toil for Christ and reap in joy.
Oh! love transcendent, that for such an end
Dost smite the labourer, banish him his toil,
And take him to the Wilderness awhile.
Be comforted, my soul:—the blow is hard,
But every stroke that brings a tear is good;
To weep is thine, thine own appointed work
When voice is hushed and sickness lays thee low.
Yea, this thy sowing-time. Then broadcast sow,
Sow beside all the waters that come in
As though to drown thee; Christ the Lord is nigh
To lower or raise the stream, in love to guide;
Thy work is His, the toil and reaping too;

With Him together we rejoice; and He
Will never let His work dishonoured be.
Joy in thy sorrow then, my suffering soul,
Count it all joy by suffering thus to learn;
Sow broadcast of the word, drink deep the fount
Of springing life, break up each clod of earth
That can obstruct the seed's full energy;
Rich harvest is for thee of grace and power
Of strength and comfort from this silent work.
For others thou art gathering: when once
The hand is full and ready to be used,
Thou shalt go out, rejoicing to cast forth
The bread that thou hast gained, full far and wide,
And bring fresh sheaves of glory to the Saviour's side.

XXIV.

ADVENT.

AMID the darkness that surrounds us,
  And the Heaven's thunder-cleavings,
Amid the terrors that confound us
  At the earth's distinct upheavings,
What the increasing gleam of brightness
That fills the air with balmy lightness?
Lo! 'tis the coming of my Lord and Master,
Would, would that I could speed it faster!

He comes; and this our world's transgression
Bids us first of judgment think,
While conscience uttering her confession
Stands upon destruction's brink;
But not so faith, with her glad leadings,
She well remembers Jesu's pleadings,
Then hears glad voices of a Saviour sing,
And fain would speed His Advent's wing.

The Saviour comes; no more to suffer,
No more to die upon the cross,
No more salvation's gift to offer
Through trial, suffering, and loss;
He comes to take His ransomed bride
And place her by His glorious side;
And I too, if I patiently abide Him,
Shall have my happy place beside Him.

Glad welcome then to every sorrow
That seems to tell of shade and night,
There must be soon a bright to-morrow,
Methinks I see its early light;
"When troubles thicken," Jesus said,
"My people, then lift up your head,
"It is the sign that your redemption draweth nigh,
"Abide, abide it patiently."

Thrice blessed prospect of redemption!
  Well may it fill the heart with gladness!
For 'tis the promise of exemption
  From all that chills our life of sadness;
Yea, 'tis the presence of the Saviour
Omnipotent with love and favour;
He comes: let heaven and earth prepare His throne,
He comes to triumph in His own.

And I am His, and He is mine,
  I know it by the love I feel,
Through Him my gleams of mercy shine,
  To Him my heart makes fond appeal:
Come, come, thou long-desired Master,
Speed on Thy chariot-wheel yet faster,
Prepare the nations, be Thy church's Saviour,
And take Thy Throne, O King, for ever.
  NICE, 1860.

XXV.

"Wherefore glorify God in the fires." (Isaiah xxiv. 15.)

TIME of anguish, time of sorrow,
  'Tis no time for mortal praise,
Some other mould the sufferer must borrow
  Ere he can sing as in his happier days.

But who asks it? not our *Father*,
He who every trial sends,
He mocks not our sufferings, but the rather
For every sorrow gracious succour lends.

Jesus asks not; for He knoweth
Full too well the suff'rer's part;
His loving sympathy the wider groweth,
As each new sorrow tries His servant's heart.

The *Spirit* asks not; for He's waiting
To be graciously employed,
With His own blessèd comforts compensating
For every toil, and most when unalloyed.

Nor is praise what God requires,
'Tis not tempted that we sing;
To "glorify the Lord within the fires,"
This is the tribute that He bids us bring.

His blessèd *Name* to glorify,
God of Mercy, God of Grace;
And this His child can do in every cry
By looking up to Him with smiling face.

His *Work of Love* to glorify;
  Lowly patience, simple faith,
By these the suffering soul can best reply
  To all that doubting world or tempter saith.

His own *Dear Son* to glorify,
  Saviour most in trial's hour;
Prove it by drawing from His rich supply,
  And all around will feel the gracious power.

Oh! for the grace to glorify
  Jesus' love within the fires;
Praise shall be sung to all eternity,
  When joy in God fulfils the soul's desires.

XXVI.

CHRISTMAS DAY.

Ah! gladdest of all glad—the night
That shepherds crowned with angels' light,
Far brightest of all bright the morn
That said, "To us a child is born."
'Tis Host of Heaven that enraptured sing
Redemption's glory messengers to bring.

Age on Age was quickly passing,
Wo on wo unchecked amassing,
When the glad tidings broke from heav'n,
"To us, to us a son is given;"
Well might the earth with glowing rapture swell
And rival angels in the joy they tell.

The King of Kings the manger holds,
Jesus Bethlehem's stall enfolds,
Immanuel in the flesh is seen,
A glory that had never been;
Whose tongue could silent be? whose heart refuse
Its burst of gladness at the welcome news?

Yes, all shall sing the blessed story:
Tell we henceforth Immanuel's glory,
We triumph in that lowly birth,
As sharing e'en the worst of earth;
"To us a child is born, to us a son,"
That we with Jesus may be ever one.

Then carry on the joyful tiding,
For 'tis "the Wonderful" abiding,
"Counsellor and God Almighty,
"The Father of Eternity,
"The Prince of Peace:" go tell His love to men,
And bid the nations visit Bethlehem.

There too we still each throb of sadness,
There rest we every hope of gladness,
Mercy and Truth together met,
Who shall not there his woes forget?
To Bethlehem's manger every sorrow bring,
And learn of angels how for aye to sing.

NICE, 1860.

XXVII.

CLOSE OF YEAR.

WHY do we love in evening hours
To watch the sun in its decline,
To trace it as it gently lowers
Beyond our vision's boundary-line?

Is it that, softest colours blending
Their wondrous changes o'er the scene,
We feel th' enchantment they are lending
To hill and dale and each ravine?

'Tis that the eyes more calmly fasten
On forms of shadow than of light,
Entranced to view them as they hasten
Or lengthen to embrace the night.

'Tis that the soberer tones of feeling
  Are most congenial to the mind,
And these their furtherance or healing
  In twilight's solemn moments find.

Who knows not that these moments wake
  Our memories of time gone by,
Though dim and dark, as they partake
  Of all around insensibly?

Who knows not the mysterious power
  That hangs o'er twilight's fading path,
As telling of a coming hour
  Of world-wide darkness and of wrath?

The present all so fitly shown
  In briefest glory, then in shade,
Naught of the next brief moment known,
  But that it lives to shine and fade.

Such story does the twilight tell;
  And we, the creatures of a day,
Must needs, as fleeting, like full well
  Such ending of our sunlit way.

But oh! if thus by evening taught
  Of doubting hope or trusting fear,
How shall not every deepest thought
  Be wakened by the closing year?

Not the declining of a sun,
  But earth gone down in wintry sadness;
A twelvemonth's course completely run
  Of joy and sorrow, woe and gladness:

Not the mere colours softly blending
  Their transient beauties all around,
But Nature very sternness lending
  To earth and sky, to sea and ground:

Not the mere lengthening of the shade,
  And filling up each gleam of light,
But summer long since seen to fade,
  And all enwrapped in folds of night:

Not wakened memories dimly traced,
  Not kindling soberer tones of feeling,
But life, in all its period faced,
  To conscience as its judge appealing.

The past, a chain that, link by link,
  Connects us with a world unseen,
And we, just standing on the brink,
  The creatures we have ever been:

Each sin upon our spirit graven,
  Each mercy noted in its birth,
Marked is each breath of love from Heav'n
  Just as it touched some spot of earth:

And every day so marked and known!
  Each moment heav'nly tokens wearing!
Sure 'tis not memory wakes alone,
  But all stand out their record bearing:

Each year and month and day and hour
  Has its own plainly written features,
And closing years tell out with power
  These claims of God on all His creatures.

The closing year! 'tis life just ending,
  Periods such as this forecast,
A closing world still more portending
  The day of judgment nearing fast.

What heart, then, at this solemn season
  Beats not responsive to its teaching?
Why, 'tis the soul's best act of reason
  To present, past, and future reaching.

And oh! if reason thus direct us
  In thoughts of solemn doubt to share,
How should not faith and love affect us
  Beholding mercy everywhere?

Behold we this, and twilights tell
  Unnumbered truths to memory dear,
Beholding this we love to dwell
  On every closing of the year.

Another year in mercy granted!
  Another year with blessings fraught!
Why, 'tis an angel's tongue that's wanted
  To tell the story as we ought.

But see how words will come apace
  To fill a grateful Christian's page,
When he detects the Saviour's face
  As shining on his pilgrimage.

Mark we the past by frequent losses?
  Each month and week its trial bears?
A Saviour's hand then points to crosses
  As God's best antidote to fears.

There's naught so dark but what is brightened
  By that true glory from above,
There's not a woe but must be lightened
  By gleams from that unending love.

Is Nature's face enwrapped in gloom?
  The winter does but nourish spring;
In cold the flowers gain strength to bloom;
  And lengthened frosts best harvests bring.

The sun goes down to rise again;
  In Christ the loved ones sleep to wake;
Things dark shall at His word be plain,
  His heaviest clouds in mercy break.

For what of sin? 'tis all forgiven,
  When souls are cleansed in Jesus' blood;
The World unseen? His purchased Heav'n
  Is just beyond death's chilling flood.

The future, whether joy or sorrow,
  Is all fore-known and well-arranged;
And He that holds the unknown morrow
  A purpose of His love ne'er changed.

Then what if years go down in dulness?
  The sunshine must be seen awhile;
We draw but from the Saviour's fulness
  And all around is seen to smile.

Our days and years, our life and death,
  Our every time is in His hand,
And He, who gave our earliest breath,
  Our life of glory shall command.

Then live we for His glory here,
  By faith beholding that above,
And banishing each shade of fear
  Bask in the sunshine of His love.

NICE, 1860.

XXVIII.

"My times are in thy hand." (Psalm xxxi. 15.)

My times in Thy Hand, Lord,
There would I have them be,
All rests on Thy good word,
Nothing depends on me.

Times of my sickness, each
From Thy favour meted,
All sent in love to teach
The soul's health completed:

My times of suffering
So well arranged by Thee,
My clouds of sorrowing
Bursting so carefully:

Times of yet deeper woe,
By Satan invested,
For trial come and go
By Thy mercy tested:

No drop is unbrightened
By light of love divine,
Each burthen is lightened
By Jesus fixed as mine:

Times of my greatest joy,
  By Thee apportioned,
Meet their exact alloy,
  Heart from Thee cautioned:

My streams of pure blessing
  Flow fast from the mountain,
Thy hand so well pressing
  Each drop from the fountain.

Faith, love, and every grace
  From Thy great mercy spring,
Salvation's time and place
  Thou dost, O Father, bring.

What then the thing of earth
  That can the mind enthral,
If it derive its birth
  From Him who knoweth all?

Sure it is well to leave
  All to a Father's care;
Much less a Christian grieve
  Aught at His word to share.

Times are all best for me
  Thus by the Lord arranged;
What a true rest for me
  When things by Him are changed!

Naught shall disturb my heart,
  Trusting my all above,
God's purpose none can thwart,
  None stay His perfect love.

That love I know is mine
  By Jesus' gift to me,
His arms my life entwine,
  Saviour eternal He.

His times my own for aye,
  My times His supplying,
Life or death, night or day,
  On Him all relying,

His will, my soul, await,
  Leave all to His command,
And during life repeat,
  "My times are in Thy Hand."

NICE, *January* 1*st*, 1861.

XXIX.

"I go to prepare a place for you." (John xiv. 2.)

"Many Mansions," Home of Glory,
Jesus thither gone before!
Christian pilgrims, homeward soar ye,
Soon you'll have to wait no more.

"Father's House," name how endearing!
Heritage of Sons of God!
Suffering Christian, heart be cheering,
Soon you'll reach your own abode.

What can keep us from its blessing?
Jesus now prepares our place;
Banish every thought distressing,
At the bidding of His grace.

Wait in patience Jesus' coming
To Himself to take His own,
In the distance there is looming
Vision of the Coming One.

Ever ready once believe Him
To prepare us for our place,
Making ready to receive Him
We shall see Him face to face.

XXX.

"Make me to know mine end, and the measure of my days, what it is; that I may know how frail I am."

(Bible Version, Psalm xxxix. 4.)

Is it, O Lord, too much to ask of Thee,
  To let me know my end?
How great the measure of my days may be
  To ask is not t'offend?

Forgive me then if I would seek to know
  When Thou my soul wilt call;
'Tis not that I unwilling am to go,
  Trusting to Thee my all.

Faith bids me rest assured that all my days
  Will have their blessing given,
The past confirms th' assurance that my ways
  Are registered in Heaven.

But yet I ask Thee; for behold my aim
  My frailty is to see,
To know what grace and mercy I must claim
  For all my life from Thee.

So uniform Thy loving-kindness, Lord,
  So constant Thy kind care,
That I am led sometimes to think Thy Word
  Is passed for resting here.

And Thou, Lord, knowest that I would not rest
Here in the world below,
A world whose hopes and pleasures stand confess'd
Inheritors of woe.

To burst the bands that fetter me to earth
My heaven-born spirit pines,
I've learned to value at its proper worth
Whate'er the soul confines.

And hence my frailty I desire to learn
How soon these earth scenes close,
For thus in every time to Thee I turn
For labour or repose.

XXXI.

"Lord, let me know mine end and the number of my days: that I may be certified how long I have to live."
(Prayer Book Version, Psalm xxxix. 5.)

Yes! 'tis a weak conceit to ask to know
The end of life how near,
Since plenteous streams of loving kindness flow
Unceasing year by year.

Enough for me that it is fixed and known
By Him who orders all,
By one who, saving, loves to make His own
Whate'er may us befal.

Perchance it might be pleasant to take count
Of time yet left to me,
And seem to calculate the full amount
Of life's activity.

So many labours might be undergone
In hope their end to see;
"'Tis finished" might be said of everyone
Of works begun by me.

The whole life brought within its proper space
As far as man could tell,
And I look up with a contented face
For service done full well.

But oh! what weight of trouble would be mine
To fill life's proper scene!
How would my spirit oftentimes repine
For what my life has been!

I leave it now in loving Mercy's hand,
Its end and space unknown,
I rest each breath upon my Lord's command,
And call not one my own:

My labours, scanty though they be, are done
Because I love my Lord,
Their power developed, as it was begun,
For He doth grace afford.

And life thus sought from Him is ever sure
Its purpose to fulfil,
Because His mercy cannot but endure
To make it work His will.

Not I, but Christ, is living evermore,
In Christ I live my day;
And if beyond my heart and spirit soar
'Tis on the Heav'nward way.

That home may e'en be mine before to-morrow,
And then my labours cease;
There the true end of patience, as of sorrow,
Life's end unending peace.

The very thought of what the Lord may do
Enkindles flame of love,
It makes me on my toilsome way to go
Enlightened from above.

One thing is certain, "all uncertain here,"
And this for us is best,
Our souls are kept in a believing fear,
That here is not our rest.

That rest we seek on each succeeding day,
Depending on God's word,
To Him commit each portion of our way,
His own in Christ the Lord.

No anxious thought, but simple faith, we give
  To Him who is life's giver;
We're certified how long we have to live,
  "Henceforth with Christ for ever."

XXXII.

"And what hast thou that thou didst not receive?"
(1 Cor. iv. 7.)

If aught should rest on thee alone,
There's naught, O man, to call thine own:
  Of all things present, all things past,
    Thine to receive,
    'Tis God's to give
  The smallest blessing that thou hast.

Thy life is fairly judged to be
A something that belongs to thee,
  And yet which day, or even hour?
    Thine the living,
    God's the giving
  Thy breath and all thy vital power.

The weary limbs demand repose,
With sweetest sleep thine eyelids close,
  Yet when begin and wherefore cease?
    Thine the sleeping,
    God's the keeping
  His own beloved in rest and peace.

The morning calls thee to arise,
Refreshed the frame at once complies,
  Yet whence the vigour to obey?
    Thine the waking,
    God's the making
  The term, the light, the life of day.

Thou hast delights beyond the telling,
Ah! 'tis thy tide of life-blood swelling,
  But whose the ocean of the love?
    Thine the joying,
    God's th' employing
  The winds, the springs, that waters move.

Is sorrow thine appointed lot,
And stranger intermeddleth not?
  Yet whence the fountain of thy tears?
    Thine the mourning,
    God's th' adorning
  With dew thy little world of fears.

Or hast thou struggles sore and lengthened
For each of which thy soul is strengthened?
  Who gives the issue of the fight?
    Thine the contest,
    Christ's the conquest,
  And God the Author of thy might.

When all thy trials are endured,
Thy warfare ended, peace secured,
What else remains for thee below?
Thine the dying,
God's th' applying
The perfect cure of all thy woe.

He calls thee to thy future home,
Then gives thee life and power to come,
Thy crown, by whom the triumph won?
Thine for ever,
For God never
Has left His gracious work undone.

Thy future with the Angels shared,
Thy place by Jesus well prepared,
'Tis thine the mercy to explore,
Thine the story,
God's the glory,
Oh! be it His for evermore.

XXXIII.

"Consolation abounds." (2 Cor. i. 5.)

And what thy *sufferings*, man of many *woes?*
"Greater than I can bear,"
Not if they come from One who loving knows
His servants everywhere.

Thy power to resist and to endure
He knows it all full well;
He deals the blow according to the cure,
'Tis healing, not a spell.

What thy *desert*, O man of many *sins?*
"Far greater than my pain;"
This then the way whereby the Lord begins
To make thee glad again.

His dispensation wilt thou not receive
So plainly one of love?
He must afflict thee ere He can relieve,
And so affection prove.

What are thy *blessings*, man of many *joys?*
"Divine and numberless;"
Behold the means a God of love employs
To make thy tongue confess.

He makes thee draw the contrast, and compare
Thy present with the past;
How short the time and space for sorrows are
While heavenly blessings last.

What of *Another's sufferings*, man *redeemed*,
Jesus, thy Saviour Lord?
No suff'rings terrible shall now be esteemed,
Silenced is every word.

Wilt liken thine to His? thou must expect
The very dregs to drink,
The cup He gives thee thou canst not reject
However strength may sink.

Then take thine own, it is enough for thee,
Sufficient for the day;
Let Him in trial thy deliverer be,
And leave to Him the way.

He knows from deep experience the weight
That each of us can bear;
He lives to succour our afflicted state,
No less than joys to share.

XXXIV.

"For even hereunto were ye called." (1 Peter ii. 21.)

Garb of mourning,
Life of scorning,
Both by Jesus' suffering brought;
Loath to wear it?
Hard to bear it?
This is not a Christian thought.

Earth's clay soiling,
Sin's despoiling,
  Curse of an o'erburthened race;
Not to expect it
Or reject it,
  This is not the fitting place.

Toil and trouble,
Yea, their double,
  Has not God appointed thee?
How refuse them,
When to use them
  Christ himself anointed thee?

Courage sinking,
Nature shrinking,
  Such the fears that spirit move?
Grace abounding
Sin confounding,
  Surely thou wilt victor prove.

Years are passing,
Fears amassing
  At the near approach of death;
Rather mend them
As we spend them,
  Bless'd thereby is every breath.

Comes there trial,
Or denial
  Of the work we try to do?
Blessings given,
Such in heaven
  Shall we trace their lessons true.

Not a heart-fear,
Not an eye-tear,
  But it bears some good to thee:
There's not an ill
But marks God's will,
  And 'tis wisdom this to see.

XXXV.

"There is a river, the streams whereof shall make glad the city of God." (Psalm xlvi. 4.)

Who but can tell the exquisite delight,
That bursts upon his spirit at the sight
Of some bright peaceful river, nestling deep,
As though reclining on its grassy steep?

Sweet tranquil stream, unruffled by the sound
Of life's sad turmoil, or the giddy round
Of worldly pleasures, that enchantment lose
So quickly by the absence of repose.

Methinks no heart could unrefined remain
By meditation on that peaceful scene ;
The thirst for beauty natural to man
Invites to joy when called such scene to scan.

What joy again to traveller so great
As, thirsting in the desert, streams to meet !
How fainting courage rises at the sight,
And limbs refreshed regain their wonted might !

As deep the murmurs of the chosen host,
Their faith mid wilderness-exhaustion lost,
So raised their hopes, so bright their sunlit gleam,
When smitten rock supplied the living stream.

Beleaguered city, perishing with thirst,
May well its barrier despairing burst,
One hope excited of that want's supply,
See how it warms them into constancy.

Nor otherwise with Zion, city pure,
Its walls salvation, and its strength secure,
A city yet beleaguered, in distress,
Its foes, by Satan marshalled, numberless.

No need, however, in this sure abode,
In this our Zion, city of our God,
To doubt rich its abundance, or despair
Of ample streams of living water there.

There is a river, and its peaceful course
Is borne unsullied from its Heav'nly source,
The streams whereof make glad the heart of all
That rest undoubting in that city's wall.

No thirst of needing spirit unsupplied,
No strength for battle from the stream denied,
Joy to the doubting, peace to troubled souls,
The stream such blessings on its bosom rolls.

No toil of enemy, nor yet device,
Has e'er prevailed to injure its supplies:
Let but the want be felt, the mercy sought,
Some copious channel to the soul is brought.

Blest stream of joy unceasing! river bright
With gleams of sunshine from the Saviour's light!
Type of the fulness destined to arise
When man redeemed shall enter Paradise!

Oh! if to view the earthly scene be peace,
The cure of sorrow, or from sin release;
If sight of nature's beauty so enthral
The eye, the spirit, and the heart of all:

If traveller gain his courage from the sight
Of stream in desert and from draught his might;
If smitten rock each murmur drove away
That Israel's blessings seemed awhile to stay:

If city thirsting, compassed with the foe,
Find every hope return as waters flow;
Shall not the christian-heart with triumph rise
To tell unbidden Zion's rich supplies?

This be its glory that we haste to speak,
This be the fountain that we love to seek;
The hand to draw, the thirst to feel aright,
Be these, O Lord, the offspring of thy might!

XXXVI.

"Looking unto Jesus." (Heb. xii. 2.)

Why refuse, my soul, to bear it
Whatsoe'er the burthen be?
'Tis not well for thee to fear it,
When so much is borne for thee:
Jesus bore it,
Canst thou then refuse to bear?

Be it thorn-crown which is offered,
Place it on a patient brow,
Grace abundant, it is proffered,
Yea, His own He gives thee now:
Jesus wore it,
Wilt thou not rejoice to wear?

Is the heart full sad and weary,
By the fiery furnace tried?
Is the way so long and dreary
That all comfort seems denied?
Christ dejected,
Surely thou should'st never mourn.

Friends of early days have left thee,
Thou hast now to walk alone;
Death of dear ones has bereft thee,
And thy mainstay it is gone:
Christ rejected,
Wilt thou fear to be forlorn?

Sorely tempted is thy spirit
To rebel against the Rod?
Trial, it is thine inherit,
Promised by the living God:
Jesus proved it,
What could greater comfort give?

Dost thou now despair of reaching
That which He prepares, thy home?
Wilt thou never cease beseeching
For salvation yet to come?
Jesus loved it,
Who can make thee cease to live?

Courage, Christian, be thou pressing
O'er the ruggedness of way,
All that can be soul-distressing
Has but its appointed day:
Jesus shares it,
Thou wilt not refuse to share.

Let not faith nor hope be failing,
Sure defence and aid thine own,
Triumph is the fight entailing,
Cross shall lead thee to the crown:
Jesus wears it,
Thine He'll give thee soon to wear.

XXXVII.

"Commit thy way unto the Lord; trust also in Him; and He shall bring it to pass." (Psalm xxxvii. 5.)

And is thy way so very dark
That thou wouldst gladly find some spark
Of light whereby to guide thy bark?
Commit it to the Lord:

His footsteps they are in the sea,
His way o'er waters known to be,
And He will soon deliver thee,
If thou wilt trust His Word.

Or is it pathway hedged with thorn,
Thy garments every step are torn,
Thy feet so sadly bruised and worn?
Commit to Christ thy way.

The thorny paths He had to tread
From earth that on to glory lead;
Then He has felt the utmost need
Of thy most painful day.

Or is it journey wet with tears,
Which life so naturally bears?
Without are toils, within are fears?
Commit to Christ thine all.

He deigned to weep o'er Lazarus' grave;
The city that He longed to save,
Salvation spurned, His tears should have,
In prospect of its fall.

So tried and troubled, will not He
Thy timely aid rejoice to be,
Thy need His all-prevailing plea
If thou wilt on Him rest?

Deserted is thy way, forlorn,
An object of the worldling's scorn?
And nothing left thee but to mourn?
He, too, was oft distressed.

Commit then to the Lord thy way,
Yea, trust Him as thy lifelong stay,
Thy joy, thy light in dreariest day,
And He will comfort prove:

Commit to Him thy soul, thine all,
He guides the trials that befal,
Ere long He will thy spirit call
To share His throne of love.

XXXVIII.

"Fear thou not; for I am with thee: be not dismayed; for I am thy God: I will strengthen thee; yea, I will help thee; yea, I will uphold thee with the right hand of My righteousness." (Isaiah xli. 10.)

Scarce will the trembling child refuse
Its courage as before to gather,
When once it finds that it can use
The known protection of a Father.

Shall less the well-taught pilgrim here
Encourage faith in trouble's hour,
The promise from the Lord once given,
"I'm with thee, sufferer, in power!"

Yea, 'tis command, not promise merely,
"Fear not, thy God is at thy side,
"Be not dismayed, thy God is near thee
"Prepared to succour and abide;

"What need of thine too great for Me?
"My hand is shield from every harm;
"Thy Father, He will strengthen thee,
"Yea, help thee with His mighty arm;

"'Tis Sin that bids thy courage fail,
"So sure its punishment in wrath,
"My Righteousness shall then avail
"T' uphold thee in the narrow path."

Hear thus th' Almighty speak in love,
What heart shall courage fail to gather?
Instinct with life the dying move
At such a call from loving Father.

Nor less my soul within me burns
Its resting-place of faith to find,
Instinctively to Jesus turns
As mirror of the Father's mind.

In opened page of Inspiration
Of all that Jesus did I read;
And thereby banish my temptation
To chilling fear or childlike dread.

XXXIX.

PSALM XXIII.

"The Lord my Shepherd, every want supplied,
In pastures green He maketh me to lie,
He leadeth me pure silent streams beside,
To soul restoring former energy:
Himself my guide He condescends to make
In holy paths for His own glory's sake."

What saith the soul to mercy such as this?
Can tongue find utterance worthy such a gift?
'Tis faith to comprehend it must arise,
And grace itself the heart to speak must lift:
But such a tribute ne'er shall wanting be
From souls so taught and led so lovingly.

Then hear their language, "Though I walk the vale
Of death's chill shadow, I shall feel no ill,
For Thou art with me; Rod and Staff prevail,
As they are ever wont, to comfort still:
In face of foes my table is prepared,
The cup of oil and blessing never spared."

Faith for the Future, whatsoe'er it be,
Learn thus, my soul, thy confidence to tell,
"Goodness and mercy sure shall follow me,
How long soe'er on this cold earth I dwell;
While in Thy House for ever by Thy Grace,
Dear Lord and Shepherd, shall I see Thy face."

XL.

"I know their sorrows." (Exodus iii. 7.)

"I KNOW their Sorrows"—Oh! what precious thought
To make the tempted soul submissive lie!
And coming from the Lord who, dying, bought
That soul, bespeaks undying sympathy.

"I know their Sorrows"—How it blunts the edge
Of sharpest weapon e'en in Satan's hand,
The answer to whate'er he may allege,
Or weary sufferer's sinking faith demand.

"I know their Sorrows"—Suffereth knoweth none
In origin, continuance, or end;
In earliest strife he thinks the battle won,
And deems it ended when he learns to bend.

"I know their Sorrows"—Blessing, end, and aim,
To man unknown, to God all fully known;
Why cast we then on self the need or blame,
When we may cast our all on God alone?

"I know their Sorrows"—'Tis as though He said,
"Leave all in faith that appertains to thee,
Thy every want and needs-be shall be fed
Out of the fulness treasured up in Me."

"I know their Sorrows"—Hence whate'er the pain,
My Heavenward way rejoicing will I go,
One truth my own, sufficient to constrain,
"What now I know not, God doth fully know.'

XLI.

"Could ye not watch with me one hour." (Matt. xxvi. 40.)

WHO, who can tell, what hand can trace
The sorrows of Gethsemane?
Though seeing in the Saviour's face
Some tokens of His agony?

So dimly do those drops reflect
The world-wide sorrow that was there,
They serve to bid us recollect,
But not to weigh, one single tear.

Or who can comprehend the prayer,
A Son's petition, and in vain?
"If possible, in mercy spare
The world redeemed its dying pain:

"On me its sorrows shall descend,
For I will make them ever Mine;
Yea, I will bear them to the end,
The cup I drink, My will is Thine."

Was ever sorrow like to His?
  Yet this is not the agony;
Ye passers by, declare, is this
  The Wonder of Gethsemane?

Ah! no, there is a deeper spring
  Of sorrow to the suffering Lord,
His own belov'd the burthen bring,
  And pierce Him with the sharpest sword.

I look around and see how near
  The traitor hands that deepest wound;
His chosen friends, o'ercome with fear,
  Are stretched asleep upon the ground.

Their loving master had required
  One simple duty at their hand;
"Here tarrying watch," He had desired;
  "Yea, watch with Me," was His command.

"What! could ye not with Me one hour
  Keep watch?" we hear the Saviour say;
"Unmindful of the Heavenly power
  That makes the weakest to obey?"

No—they had failed, and failing own
  There is for man with Christ no place;
The winepress He must tread alone,
  And none can share His suff'ring Grace.

He fain would have some friendly voice,
  If not in praise, to cheer in prayer;
But that, which angels would rejoice,
  Poor sinful men refuse to share.

Themselves dependant on the woe
  That agonized His bleeding heart,
Invited to partake, they show
  How little fit to bear their part.

Their own soon coming, what shall stay
  Their sinking souls in that dread hour?
They slept the suff'ring time away
  That would have shown in Christ their power.

'Twas this their loss which deepest moved
  The tear-drops of His agony,
For by His dearest ones it proved
  Rejection of His sympathy.

Here was the spring of bitterest tear
  That could bedew the Saviour's eye,
Here were the Cup, the Thorn, the Spear,
  All meeting in Gethsemane.

Thou blessed Saviour! Suffering Lord!
  We plead Thine agonies unknown,
And look, dependant on Thy Word,
  For grace to watch from Thee alone.

XLII.

THE CROSS OF JESUS.—GOOD FRIDAY.

CROSS of Jesus! Cross of *Glory!*
Who shall stand within its Light?
Only they who know the story
Taught of Heav'n its wondrous might;
Angels, they alone, may claim the place,
The Heavenly Glory seeing face to face.

Cross of Jesus! Cross of *Blessing!*
Who shall venture near its shade?
Only they who sin-confessing
At its foot their sins have laid;
These burthened ones may claim the place
As called to share th' abundance of its grace.

Cross of Jesus! Cross of *Scorning!*
Are they all revilers there?
None to heed the solemn warning
That is echoed everywhere?
One rightly calls Him of the Jews the King,
But they in mockery His honours bring.

Cross of Jesus! Cross of *Anguish!*
Some there were that ventured near,
Hope itself constrained to languish
Yet their love could conquer fear;
One loved disciple and some women there,
With Jesus' mother sorrows came to share.

Cross of Jesus! Cross of *Sorrow!*
Sure no fear can keep away
Hearts that every joy must borrow
From the curse of Calvary;
Sin-burthened ones, or from the burthen freed,
By Jesus' Cross we lay our utmost need.

Cross of Jesus! Cross of *Trial!*
None but He, the Lord could bear!
Who shall weigh the stern denial
Of a Father's presence there?
Jesus groaned beneath that weight for me,
Can I to Him deny my sympathy?

Cross of Jesus, of *Salvation!*
All constrains to keep me nigh,
Fears of righteous condemnation,
Love, and faith, and sympathy;
Come heavy-laden sinner, friend or foe,
The Cross of Jesus welcome has for you.

Cross of Jesus! Cross of *Power!*
I would ever cling to Thee;
Thine was the appointed hour—
All was done to ransom me:
Then may I feel that all, or gain, or loss,
Is light or shadow from the Saviour's Cross.

NICE, 1862.

XLIII.

THE SAVIOUR IN THE GRAVE.—EASTER EVE.

THE night is quickly passing,
The day begins to dawn,
But heavy clouds are massing
In brief delay of morn:
No better type afforded
The Christian Church could have—
Of what this day recorded,
"The Saviour in the Grave."

'Twas thus in contemplation
I watched the break of day,
The one in the creation
When true light is away:

The very day that Satan
  Chief power might claim to have,
For he prevailed to fasten
  "The Saviour in the Grave."

Sweet sleep had comfort brought me
  Though waking in distress,
No wonder I bethought me,
  "Jesus was comfortless:"
Mine eyelids are not closing,
  The light of life I have,
While I'm on love reposing
  "My Saviour's in the Grave."

Though earth when He was dying
  In darkness seemed to shrink,
The rocks to graves replying,
  And Heaven itself to sink,
Night closes, and how surely
  The days their sunrise have,
While all returns securely
  "The Saviour's in the Grave."

Day dawns, and though clouds linger
  There's brightness in the sky,
Say is not this the harbinger
  Of blessings from on High?

Full blaze of mid-day clearness
  The earth then joys to have,
Can this be claim of nearness
  "To th' Saviour in the Grave?"

Yes, fearful heart, earth's blessing
  Must drive Thee to the tomb,
And well t'will aid thy pressing
  To th' Eternal Home;
Thou see'st there the true King
  Omnipotent to save,
To triumph best remaining
  "A Saviour in the Grave."

What thou would'st most be fearing,
  The awful power of Death,
The Lord of Life is bearing,
  And thus He comforteth:
In Satan's darkest dwelling
  He claims His power to save,
The foe for us repelling
  "As Saviour in the Grave."

No contrast then be making
  Between His state and thine,
The rather all be taking
  His life and death combine:

For thee He loved to bear it
  Thy ruined soul to save;
The Crown, Oh! let Him wear it,
  "The Saviour in the Grave!"

The earth redemption needed,
  Its soil so stained with sin,
The Saviour more than pleaded,
  He closed Himself within:
Well may remotest nations
  Proclaim His power to save,
And show to generations
  "The Saviour in the Grave."

Much more should the Redeemèd
  With sorrow mingle joy,
On day by Church esteemèd
  Best fit for such employ—
Yes! wait not for the morrow
  To tell His power to save,
Sing now with joy and sorrow
  "The Saviour in the Grave."

NICE, 1861.

XLIV.

"The Lord is risen indeed." (Luke xxiv. 34.)

EASTER DAY.

Where now thy Victory, O silent Grave?
  Brief while thou hadst the power to retain
Thy Lord and Master: He who came to save
  Could scarce be holden by thy strongest chain:
Thy Bonds are burst, for naught could e'er impede
Thy Victor's path, "The Lord is risen indeed."

Come, Christian, see the place where Jesus lay,
  How vain the soldier-guard, the seal, the stone!
He, whom the Earth, whom Heaven and Hell obey,
  O'er all has proved His perfect victory won:
His very dying power had thus availed,
Much more His Life which Death had ne'er curtailed.

Come, see the grave of Jesus: angels there,
  Glad messengers of truth to all who come,
Their vigils keep, commissioned to declare
  How Christ for all His Saints has stripped the tomb,
And yet has left it monument of Grace
For all our sins the fitting burial place.

Yea, and for us the bands of Death were broken,
That we with Christ the Lord might joyful rise,
The burial of our sins the blessed token
That hearts' affections centre in the skies ;
In Christ arisen, where He is we are,
His Death, His Life, so blessed by Him to share.

"The Lord is risen, the Lord is risen indeed,"
Would that my life the blessed truth might tell!
When once the Soul for sin has learned to bleed,
It seeks with Christ above the world to dwell;
I seek Thee, Blessed Lord, for Thou art mine,
Now raise me to Thyself, and I am Thine.

Thine now in life, and Thine, O Lord, for ever,
Thyself the first fruits of the conquered Grave,
Thine, for no power of Hell the bond can sever
Between Thee and my soul Thou cam'st to save:
Thine would I ever the glad tidings speed
"The Lord is risen, the Lord is risen indeed."

NICE, 1861.

XLV.

ASCENSION DAY.

WELL might the Saints, redeemed of old,
Bid the eternal gates unfold
  The King of Glory welcoming:
His gracious influence they knew,
And in their souls they felt it too,
  For they had bowed before the King.

The heart once taught by grace to live
Full welcome to the Lord would give,
  Then bid the world His Kingdom own:
Yea, loose the bands of Sin and Death,
Give entrance wide at every breath
  To the Divine Ascended One.

No marvel that His servants now,
Who daily at His footstool bow,
  And know His glorious triumphs gained,
Should sing of the bright sky as cleaving,
And Christ the Lord of life receiving,
  The Earth deliver'd, Heav'n attain'd.

Their souls have found a power within
Raise high their tone and conquer sin;
  What proof so sure could e'er be given
That Jesus has ascended gone
In saving glory to His own,
  Or make them know Him in the Heav'n?

"Who then is this?" if man inquire,
"That fills the heart with Heav'nly fire?"
  "The Lord of Glory," they will say;
"Who is the King and Lord of Glory?"
They can repeat at once the story,
  'Tis Christ, our life, our truth, our way.

Our guide and guard and sure protector,
Of his own Church the one director,
  So full of grace and power is He;
His precious gifts to man dispensing,
To foes their hate in recompensing,
  Has captive led captivity.

And oh! if entered into Glory,
Preparing e'en a bright place for me,
  Should not my spirit long to go?
Could I e'er doubt His promise made me,
This thought alone would now persuade me
  My Lord's ascended power to know.

But sure I need no further teaching,
For heart is ever thither reaching
  Where Christ my Lord and Saviour reigns;
His glad return my fancy paints,
With thousands of His ransomed Saints,
  And e'en myself among His trains.

Till then my soul's supreme desire
Is to attain the one step higher
  In the appointed Heav'nward way,
Fresh triumphs to my Lord to bring,
His work on earth accomplishing,
  In prospect of His Advent-day.

He comes, and nations shall confess
His power as well as righteousness,
  Their homage glad constrained to bring;
That world-regenerating hour
Shall best assert Ascension's power
  And prove Him the Eternal King.

Then hasten, Lord, the glorious day
When shades of earth shall flee away;
  Enlightened by Thy living word
The millions of our fallen race
Shall seek th' outpouring of Thy grace,
  And all shall know Thee for their Lord.

CANNES, 1861.

XLVI.

WHITSUNDAY.

SPIRIT of Life and Light,
Come with Thy *healing*,
Thine own eternal might
To us revealing;
Dying the faith that was strong in believing,
Clouded the eyes that were bright in receiving
Thy Life and Light.

Spirit of Truth Divine
Come with Thy *teaching*,
Jesus to show is Thine,
Best of heart-preaching;
Silent the tongues that were used to be speaking
The things of the Lord, and His Grace to be seeking,
Come with Thy Truth.

Spirit of Joy and Peace,
Come with Thy *blessing*,
Bring to our souls release
Tear drops suppressing;
Many the hearts that were blessed in Thy leading
By weight of affliction and sorrow are needing
Thy Joy and Peace.

Spirit of Perfect Love,
Come with Thy *guiding*,
Thou must the cold heart move
By Thine abiding;
Losing their first love, oh, how these sins abound!
In truest of Christian hearts how rarely found
Thy Perfect Love!

O Holy Spirit, Lord,
Come in Thy *fulness;*
To us reveal Thy Word;
Lighten our dulness:
Weak our convictions of sin and transgression;
Our spirit to bring to its simple confession
Is Thine, O Lord.

Spirit of Counsel Pure,
Come with Thine *aiding*,
Only by Thee is sure
Truth all-pervading:
Judgment forgotten, holiness slighted,
By Thee alone can these errors be righted,
Thy Counsel Pure.

Spirit of Heavenly Grace,
Come in Thy *Power;*
Cheer each beclouded face,
Leave us no more!
This Thine own Day, which Thy Church honours most,
Grant it to Nations a thrice-blessèd Pentecost
Of Power and Grace.

LYONS, 1861.

XLVII.

TRINITY SUNDAY

FATHER of Mercies, hear,
Sons bow before Thee;
Saviour of Mercies, hear,
Sinners adore Thee;
Spirit of Mercies, hear,
Faint ones implore Thee;
Of Mercies the Triune dispenser,
Hear us, O Hear!

'Tis Thine to create us,
Father, hast done it;
'Tis Thine to redeem us,
Saviour, hast won it;

'Tis Thine to renew us,
  Spirit, hast begun it;
      Creator, Redeemer, Renewer,
        Hear us, O Hear!

God of all Power and Might,
  Thine to support us;
Father, Son, and Spirit,
  Thine to have taught us:
Eternal Infinite,
  Thine is to comfort us:
      Almighty, Teacher, and Comforter,
        Hear us, O Hear!

O Holy, Blessed Three!
  Thy name and mark we bear:
Glorious Trinity,
  Thine own abode we are:
Perfect in Unity,
  Thy ten-fold gifts we share;
      Enlighten, constrain, and protect us,
        Hear us, O Hear!

For Thine inspiring Grace,
  Given in times of old,
We seek Thy Loving Face,
  By Jesus' dying bold;

Soul, heart, and spirit raise,
Us to Thine own self mould;
Father, Son, Holy Ghost, ever One,
Hear us, O Hear!

PARIS, 1861.

XLVIII.

"Therefore, behold, I will allure her, and bring her into the wilderness, and speak comfortably unto her. And I will give her her vineyards from thence, and the valley of Achor for a door of hope." (Hosea ii. 14, 15.)

No way of dreariness unless the Lord has made it!
No path however rugged but what Mercy laid it!
On then, Christian Pilgrim, on;
Our trials, sufferings, every one
From throne of Heaven
To us are given,
And life is all secured to us, for Christ is pledged to aid it.

And what the Wilderness that faithless hearts so dread?
The Lord allures His children in its paths to tread;
It must then have its summer bowers
Among the choicest of the flowers,
Our very own
Those flowers bloom,
And the way must needs be pleasant wheresoe'er their odours spread.

What if the Wilderness have naught in it to cheer?
No pilgrim walks therein unless the Lord be near;
His promise is for ever sure,
When He sees fitting to allure
His sons to bliss
In wilderness,
That speaking peace and comfort, He will moderate
their fear.

Her vineyards are from hence, the Christian Church
may say,
Her dreariest suff'ring nights were heralds of her day,
From persecution's bitterest hour
She gained her real world-wide power,
And so each son
By trial won
The Crown that he at Jesus' feet is privileged to lay.

Or should he over self and world no victory gain,
Nor summer vintage-draught be able to retain,
The Wilderness has yet its scope,
Achor itself is Door of Hope,
The troubled vale
Each heart may hail
As place wherein God's purpose in affliction is made
plain.

Trial a Door of Hope! O help me to discern
This gleam of light, O Lord, and I will thither turn,
With simple faith right gladly ask
For naught but my appointed task,
For Thee fulfil
Thy Righteous Will,
And trouble's choicest lesson by submission try to learn.

XLIX.

GENEVA.—COMMUNION AFTER TEN MONTHS' ABSENCE FROM PUBLIC WORSHIP.

ONCE more Thy courts, O Lord, I've trod,
Oh! with what trembling feet!
Teach me to thank Thee, O my God,
In language that is meet.

So long since praises could ascend
Thy earthly saints among,
My voice unwilling seemed to bend
In sympathetic song.

Such thoughts were crowded to my heart
Of Thy great love to me,
That I scarce knew my humble part
In Thy loved sanctuary.

One moment, 'twas the heavy Rod,
  Which chastened me so sore,
Seemed still before me, O my God,
  To bid me cease t'adore.

The next, Thy presence in the past
  Stood out so clear and bright,
It seemed a very shade to cast
  On present feebler light.

And yet my oft-expressed desire
  Was granted me to-day,
Again to join the earthly choir
  Of man's own Holy-day;

Again to hear the preached Word,
  Sweet message of Thy grace;
Again to meet th' ascended Lord
  At His own feasting-place.

Loved friends were with me, brought to seek
  Fresh cause of thanks to Thee,
And taught from the same source to speak
  The Ransomed Sinner's plea.

Why then such feeble praises mine?
  So cold my thoughts of Love?
Lord, 'tis another gift of Thine,
  That I may humbler prove:

'Tis that, as ever, I should cast
  Before Thy Throne a prayer,
For present failing, as the past,
  Its pardon gather there:

And wilt Thou not expand with fire
  This cold dull heart of stone?
Thou hast supplied th' intense desire,
  Then make it all Thine own.

Its deadness in Thine Earthly House
  In mercy, Lord, forgive;
Its powers with angel's zeal arouse,
  And all to Thee shall live.

Henceforth throughout my pilgrimage,
  Mid Saints or e'en alone,
True praise shall all my life engage,
  As sheltered by Thy Throne.

And when on earth I speak no more,
  Warmed by a purer flame
The realms of Heaven I'll explore
  To sing Thy matchless Name.

August 4th, 1861.

L.

"Thy Will be done." (Matt. xxvi. 42.)

"Thy Will, O Lord, be done,"
Thine own Beloved One
Has taught me thus, though I was loath to learn;
Obedience to Thy Will,
Let this my spirit fill,
And Tempter's deadliest shaft by grace I turn.

"Thy Will, O Lord, be done,"
'Twas hard when first begun
The contrast Thine and mine own will between;
But yet 'tis harder still
To fight against Thy Will,
Though I rejoice the struggle to have seen.

"Thy Will, O Lord, be done,"
A victory I've won
In learning thus the spirit of my King;
Thy Will, whate'er it bears,
Henceforth my soul prepares
Eternal triumph to my Lord to bring.

"Thy Will, O Lord, be done,"
'Tis language of a son
His place within Thy heart of love who knows;
Thy Will is perfect love,
Oh! may it ever prove
My joy of waking thoughts, my heart's repose!

LI.

"For in this we groan, earnestly desiring to be clothed upon with our house which is from Heaven." (2 Cor. v. 2.)

Why those tones of bitter anguish
Breaking sadly on the ear?
Hopes of Christians, do they languish,
Can their souls be racked with fear?
Surely there is some repining
In the language that we hear.

'Twere not strange that bursts of sorrow
Break from faithless hearts awhile,
Men that vainly try to borrow
Joys from earth's too treach'rous smile,
Men whose work is the confining
Hopes within what must defile.

Well may souls, when sin uprises
  Wielding its imperious sway,
Tremble at its quick surprises,
  And lament its mastery;
    See its awful curse o'erspreading
  Who but longs to be away?

Groans may well become the token
  Of a fallen prostrate race,
Evidence of spirits broken,
  Lost to all the Life of Grace;
    Utterance of wand'rers treading
  Storm-tossed in a desert place.

But shall Christian hearts be groaning
  As they wend their Heav'nward way?
Aught of their career bemoaning,
  Trav'llers in the light of day?
    Surely there is some forgetting
  Of the Sun's enlivening ray.

Burthened truly, ever toiling,
  Wounded, tried, and sadly torn,
Garments with the earth-clay soiling
  From the moment they were born,
    Soon each joy of life regretting,
  Well may soul with grief be worn.

Can such pilgrims then be singing
  Long-continued songs of praise?
Can the happiest be bringing
  Aught that tells of brighter days?
    Rather should we doubt the striking
  Of one chord for joyous lays.

Yes, though Hope and Faith be brightened
  By the presence of a Friend,
Though each trouble may be lightened
  By the knowledge of its end,
    Though the toil be to our liking,
  Or the head to burthen bend:

Look to promised Glory speeding,
  Cast one glance at future Home,
Signs of Christ's appearance heeding
  Who but thinks of joys to come?
    While the very thirst for blessing
  Casts o'er present toil a gloom.

Groans for earth's destruction coming,
  Sighs for its impenitence,
Tears for sorrows world-wide looming,
  Deep lament for man's offence,
    What but mem'ries thus oppressing
  Harass every Christian sense?

Love we Christ our Master truly,
  We must long for His return;
Serve we as His subjects duly,
  For His Kingdom we must yearn;
    Yet the more the thought is cheering
  Sin makes heart the more to burn.

Cease then at its groans to wonder,
  Lay no blame on Sorrow's cry;
When from sin we part asunder,
  Then we end our misery;
    But till then the spirit's fearing
  Justifies a tearful eye.

Rather seek the Day when Jesus
  From all eyes shall wipe the tear,
That the moment which shall free us
  From the bondage of our fear;
    Hark! the chariot-wheel approaching,
  Christ our King will soon be here.

Wait we for the perfect Dwelling
  Jesus with his loved ones shares?
Hopes of endless glory swelling
  As the Saviour's Kingdom nears,
    Welcome sorrow, toil, reproaching,
  All for Christ the Soul prepares.

LII.

"Though He slay me, yet will I trust in Him." (Job xiii. 15.)

AND is this Dying? Is it made so plain
That all thy struggles to exist are vain?
The care thou takest to prolong thy days,
The toils of healing, are they brief delays
Of what thy nature claims, the garb of death?
Well, be it so; the precious gift of breath
Is but a talent for a while thine own;
In earliest infancy the seed was sown
Of thy mortality, and if it spring—
Or e'en its ripened sheaves may seem to bring—
To harvest sooner than thy hopes allowed,
The ripening to a God of Love is owed.
He gave thee all thou hast, and what thou art
Is from the mercy He delights t'impart:
Thy sickness and thy health, thy days and age,
The first beginning of thy pilgrimage,
Thy years of growth, thy manhood's joyous prime,
And e'en the ceaseless ravages of Time,
All from His Hand are blessings freely strewn
As rays of sunlight from His Gracious Throne.
Nor less the sorrows that would seem to flow
From none but earthly source of sin-bought woe,
Thine own from sad omissions in the past,
Or worse intents which still their shadows cast;

E'en these have been permitted, and they bear
Some hidden mark of God's sustaining care:
They're part of thy probation, and their scope
Is one of warning or of solemn hope:
Thou liv'st to tell them, they are steps then gained
In life's career to show the path attained:
Time's milestones, if thou wilt, thy sorrows stand,
Their figures graven by a Master-hand:
And thou wouldst read them, yea, spell every word,
So clear the light which they themselves afford;
Nor needed is interpreter, so plain,
So legible, the lesson they contain.
"All guided by the Lord, and all portend
A future certain, an expected end:
Death marked on all, yet Life is so displayed
That in its garb all seems to be arrayed:
So blessed is Death, so life-sown is decay,
That all its terrors rise to pass away.
What then if strength be failing? Heart is sound;
Though earth should perish, there is resting-ground
For Faith, for Confidence: the very dust
Presents to thee the elements of Trust;
Death's sting long since by Jesus' death removed,
Eternal life by Resurrection proved,
Look through the mist of earth to brighter day,
Anticipate the moment of decay;
This be thy language, thy confession just,
'Yea, though He slay me, yet in God I trust.'"

LIII.

"We are willing rather to be absent from the body, and to be present with the Lord." (2 Cor. v. 8.)

FRIENDS, believe not Death's the sleeping
Of aught of ours worth the keeping,
What's immortal cannot fail;
Fading, perishing, the spirit?
Dream unreal! cease to fear it,
Death such loss can ne'er entail.

Is it loved one has been taken,
And has faith been somewhat shaken,
Fancy painting loss of all?
Active spirit prostrate lying,
Think not this to be the dying,
No such trial can befal.

'Tis mere absence from the mortal,
For the spirit Death is portal
To the House of Paradise;
Jesus' presence, this the refuge,
This th' escaping from the Deluge
Poured o'er life's infirmities.

Near the source of man's salvation.
Think ye, there can be cessation
  Of our action, of our love?
Jesus' presence when enjoying,
Then it is we're well employing
  All the springs that spirit move.

Naught is perfect here of action,
There is ever some contraction
  Of the powers we possess;
Look we, long we, for the waking
Energies for undertaking
  Perfect work of righteousness.

"Willing rather," nay, we're seeking
Jesus' presence, ever speaking
  Of the joys such hopes afford:
Dying friends to Him we give them,
Sure that He will then receive them,
  Till we follow in the Lord.

LIV.

"Wearisome nights are appointed to me." (Job vii. 3.

I'M weary of darkness, I'm weary,
  Sweet slumber my eyelids forsaking,
The night is so chilling and dreary,
  Oh! for the morning-light's breaking!

So hard to be watching and waiting
  While so slowly are passing the hours,
No pains of the body abating,
  No repose re-installing its powers.

'Tis not so with infancy's season
  Unconscious of trial or sorrow,
It would seem to be province of reason
  To be looking in pain for the morrow.

'Tis not so with him who is toiling
  Through the burthens and heat of the day,
No thoughts his repose are despoiling,
  Naught but morning drives slumber away.

Ah! would that my childhood's reposing,
  For a while could return to my aid,
My eyes gentle sleep would be closing
  As the glories of sun-setting fade:

Or would for one night, I could hide me
  Where the sleepers their weary limbs lay,
'Tis not that their labour's denied me,
  For I toil far beyond them all day.

Thus my heart in its night-watch was musing,
  And its foolish complainings arose,
The times of its trial abusing,
  And courting delay of repose.

Then again as I tossed on my pillow
  I bethought me of others that suffer,
Yea, are tossed upon life's every billow,
  And whose pathway than mine is far rougher.

What of One whose example is given
  For the comfort of all who are weary,
Not a ray of light His to enliven,
  Not a day, but was painful and dreary?

Yet, hear him, though faith seems to falter,
  He can bow in submission full lowly,
Not a step of his way would he alter,
  Howe'er it may drag dull and slowly.

What if nights of chill darkness are offered,
  And no respite from weariness given?
There's a truth he has long since discovered,
  "Not a pain but has record in Heaven."

Nay, "wearisome nights" full of sorrow
  Are "appointed" by One who knows best;
He prepares us aright for each morrow,
  And He gives or denies us His rest.

Our toils all "appointed," each trial
  Comes straightway from Him who is Lord,
From One who shows love in denial
  No less than in most loving Word.

Shall not faith then rise surer and higher
  The more wearisome night's waking hours?
Time will come when we learn to admire
  Heaven's mode of enhancing our powers.

It may seem to be harder to bear them
  The more often our trials are given,
Yet it is as though Love came to share them
  When it says they're appointed in Heaven.

Not a night-watch though painful and weary
  Henceforth shall my courage disturb;
Let my way be all darksome and dreary,
  Every thought of impatience I'll curb.

I know whom to trust, for I'm seeking
  The truths He would have me acquire,
I can leave all I have in His keeping,
  And e'en now His appointments admire.

How in ages to come I shall love them,
  Faith assures me by showing the Saviour,
'Twill be endless rejoicing to prove them
  In my Lord the best tokens of favour.

LV.

"My soul is even as a weaned child." (Psalm cxxxi. 2.)

The babe, no more impatient to derive
The strength that fondest mother loves to give,
Weaned from that source of natural supply
More passive on her breast can gently lie,
Its wants all love, its greatest joy a smile,
Whose heart to gladness would it not beguile?

And such the soul when purified, a child
Its fittest emblem, lowly, meek, and mild,
Weaned from the once-ensnaring things of earth,
Freed from its trammels by a second birth,
And yet retaining all its better love,
Things earthly hallowing by things above.

But oh! what process doth the Soul require
To wean itself from earth! The very fire
Of sorrow, sickness, trial, or of woe,
So often needed! nor one only blow,
But precept upon precept, line on line,
From the Chastising Hand of Love Divine.

For not as ivy clinging to the tree
With daily increase of tenacity,
Not as the vine its clasping tendrils throwing,
And thus by every aid that bears it growing,
But as the child on mother that depends
So clings the soul and with its succour blends.

And see what stained polluted source of strength
The soul by nature seeks, until at length
A very poison is its nourishment:
'Tis then the trial is in mercy sent;
From every sin-stained source the soul to free
And loose the burthens of humanity.

Yes, and from one's very self one needs the weaning,
From idol self—some folly we are gleaning,
Or pride, or self-opinion, or conceit,
From all the varied chances that we meet—
Prolific parent of how many an ill
That clogs the spirit and enslave the will!

The very love that kindred hearts unites,
The wife's devotion, innocent delights,
The duties undertaken, pleasures pure,
The thoughts that e'en for ages shall endure—
All objects of idolatry become,
Dethroning God and making earth a home.

How then shall He our forced affection gain,
And souls world-loving to His service train?
How but by weaning from the deadly food,
And showing that His discipline is good;
The idol He destroys, He smites in love,
He lays us low, earth's vanity to prove.

Yea, and for ever bless'd the hand that smites,
And thus His children to Himself unites!
We thank Thee, loving Father, for the blow,
Howe'er severe, that tends to lay us low:
The woe, the toil, oh! let their profit be
To make us love Thee, yea, love only Thee.

LVI.

"Thou shalt guide me with Thy counsel, and afterward receive me to Glory." (Psalm lxxiii. 24.)

GLOWING words of living Faith!
  Their very utterance cheers;
Say we what the Psalmist saith
  And who shall nourish fears?

They speak of Heav'nly guidance
  In sorrow and in joy,
They argue a reliance
  That nothing can destroy.

As said for us we take them
  And well we know we may,
Our own by faith we make them
  Instruction for our way.

What if the way be crowded
  By those we cannot love?
What if each day be clouded,
  And all is dark above?

We yet have One to guide us,
  A Counsellor and Friend,
Whatever may betide us
  His aid He hastes to lend.

Though doubts suggested harass,
  And heart itself grows cold,
Though Mighty Hosts encompass
  By past success made bold:

Our Friend is nigh to feed us
  With faith-inspiring word,
A Conqueror to lead us,
  Of Hosts the Mighty Lord.

When coward thoughts are rising,
  Encouragement He gives;
A sudden fear surprising,
  As Parent He receives.

The way seems long and dreary,
  He cheers us with a smile;
The feet are sore and weary,
  He bids us rest awhile.

His Spirit ever willing
  To help us in our need,
Our souls with comfort filling,
  He guides in very deed.

His counsel ever lending
  No darkness can betray,
Our very footsteps bending
  He well secures our way.

Then let the world be hastening
  To its appointed goal,
Let deadliest foes be fastening
  Their weapons 'gainst my soul:

Let seas be sweeping o'er me,
  And all appear opposed,
Let sorrows be before me
  And doors of hope all closed;

Let doubts and fears assail me,
  And life a burthen prove,
This Word shall never fail me,
  A message from above;

"Thou, Lord of Hosts, wilt guide me
  With counsel rightly given,
And place my soul beside Thee,
  In Glory and in Heaven."

LVII.

"He doth not afflict willingly nor grieve the children of men." (Lam. iii. 33.)

PARENT knows how deep the sorrow
In children's punishment,
Glad to banish to the morrow
The sad, though good, intent:
Yet none can tell the bitter pang our Father must endure
When He is forced to afflict His sons to bring them to their cure.

'Tis not within the Mind of Heaven
To cause unneeded woe,
Long has a loving Father striven
T'avert the coming blow:
And if in tender chastisement He must to sons cause grief,
With every blow, nay, in the rod, there comes a sure relief.

Say, suffering brother, is there not
Great comfort in the thought,
That loving-kindness sent you what
You fancied anger brought?
Nay, own your fears unfounded and all your doubts misplaced
When lines of heavy punishment, instead of love, you traced.

Nor yet by any wrong name call
Whatever may betide,
Or if affliction should befall
Its nature do not hide:
God doth afflict His loved ones, though unwilling be the blow,
And grief is grievous to the soul, and God would have it so.

'Tis only that He comforteth
When heaviest He smites,
And every son who suffereth
To rest on Him invites:
And hence with every chastisement His mercy He declares,
A heart of loving-kindness, not of anger, that He bears.

Be comforted then, sufferer,
Bear joyfully your grief,
A God of Love, not wrath, is near,
And He will bring relief:
The need of the correction is what you have to learn,
'Tis well the eye, not up alone, but innerward should turn.

LVIII.

"LOOK UP THROUGH NATURE UP TO NATURE'S GOD."

Some *Flowers* there are will ne'er exhale
Their fragrance pure and sweet,
Till torn by some Autumnal gale
Or crushed beneath the feet.

Full many a *Seed* beneath the earth
Is struggling into light,
Till some rude shock shall give it birth
Or raise th' incumbent weight.

There's not a *Tree* that takes firm hold
Of its appointed ground,
Till storms have well prepared its mould
And battered it around.

Who can employ his *Noblest powers*,
Or know their real end,
Save he who learns in struggling hours
How to resist or bend?

Hast watched the *Gold-refining fire*
That clears away the dross?
And didst thou not the work admire
Nor count the process lost?

He trusts his *Bark* upon the sea
Who knows its answering helm;
Such captain says right gallantly
That naught shall overwhelm.

And thus, my Soul, would I fain cast
Thy life on every sea,
E'en from the testing of the past,
Best proof of love to thee.

Here, here, thy strength, O needing Soul,
God sees each trial's end,
And He, who comprehends the whole,
Is thy Eternal Friend.

He knows the needs-be, and the good
Of each chastising blow;
He sat above the Deluge-flood,
And rules each tempest now.

Be sure He knows and does the best
That can be done for thee,
The trial, greatest or the least,
Is just as it should be.

Enough for thee is to attain
Full profit from the rod,
And Nature's self may teach the gain
Of pointing thus to God.

The fragrance of the foot-crushed Flower,
The Seed relieved of weight,
The Tree root-lengthening every hour,
The strength fresh brought to light;

The fire-refining of the Gold,
The ship that rides the sea,
From each of these, my Soul, be told
What trial brings to thee:

New Incense for the Lord of Heaven,
Some fresh enlivened grace,
A better hold on Jesus given,
New shining from His face;

The Dross removed, the soul more pure,
More Boldness in the way,
To these each trial should allure,
And shall do every day.

Then welcome, O my Soul, the Rod
That smites thee as a friend,
'Tis surest Mercy from thy God,
And Love its perfect end.

LIX.

"And yet I am not alone, because the Father is with Me." (John xvi. 32.)

ONE moment's anguish there must be
That mortal spirit could not bear,
The Saviour bore, and none but He,
That God His fallen sons might spare:

That moment when the crucified
In dying pains at Calvary,
With sin o'erwhelmed, "My God," he cried,
"Why, why hast Thou forsaken Me?"

And this in mercy to our race,
That none with Jesus might compare,
To show recipients of grace
Redeeming anguish none can share.

'Tis but a moment; man would fail
Were single toil unshared his own,
And so lest sorrows should prevail,
E'en Christ Himself is "not alone."

"I'm not alone in all beside
The dying throes of Calvary;"
Thus bids He every soul confide
In a loved Father's sympathy.

"I'm not alone:" a Father nigh
Sees, hears, and marks each trial sent,
Then hastes His presence to supply,
E'en in His heaviest chastisement.

"I'm not alone," then come what may,
E'en Death of loved ones premature,
The body's failure or decay,
Whate'er I'm called on to endure;

Unkindness, persecution, woe,
Or sorrows to which flesh is heir,
I'll cry aloud each step I go,
"With Christ my Lord in all I share."

LX.

"He shall sit as a Refiner and Purifier of Silver." (Malachi iii. 3.)

SHALL suffering child of man perplexed inquire
A Father's object in the furnace-fire?
Thus speaks the Word: "The trial of our faith,
More precious than of gold that perisheth,
Is found to issue in eternal praise
What moment Jesus comes His Saints to raise."

Not for the mere refining is it sent,
The Soul's perfection is the blest intent:
Not that the dross alone, the filth of clay,
Should by the furnace-heat be purged away;
'Tis that God's Image may reflected be,
And all the world His work of Glory see.

Such then the aim of the refining fire,
The Soul's attraction to the one step higher;
Nor till the work its progress due has made
Can hand of the Refiner e'er be stayed;
Not till He sees His image in the mass
Can cooling process be allowed to pass.

Hence what though fire of suffering lighted be,
Or heated sevenfold by the enemy?
Its every spark, as caught from flame above,
Reflects or magnifies the Hand of Love;
The gain perfection, and the only loss
A Father's melting of the sin-grained dross.

LXI.

"My Grace is sufficient for thee." (2 Cor. xii. 9.)

"SUFFICIENT Grace!" it is the Lord who says it,
The Mighty Conqueror Himself displays it;
He conquered for His people : I am one,
I know it by the fight long since begun;
By Grace he humbled me; when lying low
By Grace He raised me, then He bade me go
Rejoicing to have found a power within
For each new battle against every sin.
Henceforth no thorn, but what its point is broken;
No fierce assault, but 'tis of Love the token,
The trial of our patience, test if faith
Will rest upon the arm which compasseth.
"His grace sufficient," shall we dare to say
That aught obstructs us in our Heavenward way?
"Strength perfected in weakness," then the fight
Is for the honour of the Saviour's might.
Go forward, Christians, every victory gained
Is some new issue of His love explained,
In simple faith before the Throne adore ye,
And say, "If grace for grace, 'tis grace for glory."

LXII.

"Casting all your care upon Him; for He careth for you (1 Pet. v. 7.)

WHEN trouble's dark shower
Seems just ready to fall,
When coldest the night-hour,
And no aid within call,
How doth God's Mercy beam
In full daylight on me—
"Cast all thy Care on Him
For He careth for thee."

Hushed may be voice of friend,
Stilled for aye in the grave,
Help none prepared to lend,
Much less able to save,
How doth God's word then seem
Sun-light of sympathy—
"Cast all thy Care on Him
For He careth for thee."

Let there be none on earth
Seeking my happy home,
Not one whose love is worth
Trying to make my own,

Yet there is one Supreme
  Whose Word shall comfort be—
"Cast all thy Care on Him
  For He careth for thee."

The woe it doth vanish,
  Unfelt is the sorrow,
When heart can thus banish
  Its fears for the morrow;
Naught should we trial deem
  When such teaching we see—
"Cast all thy Care on Him
  For He careth for thee."

Let then what may arise,
  Woe, sickness, or trial,
Hatred of enemies,
  Or e'en friends' denial,
In night or mid-day gleam
  My song shall ever be—
"Cast all thy Care on Him
  For He careth for thee."

LXIII.

"No more sea." (Rev. xxi. 1.)

WHENE'ER I stand upon the ocean-shore,
I ask the question: "Can it be
A promise or a threat to me
That time must come when sea shall be no more?"

Sure evidence of a Creator's power,
The mirror wherein best to prove
The reflex of Almighty Love,
Oh! can it be that this shall be no more?

Who can forget his first, though childhood's, view
Of mighty ocean? How the soul
Then bounded to embrace the whole!
And yet e'en still each look brings something new.

So, too, when separated for a while—
Just as with welcome fond we greet
The friends that we may chance to meet—
So dear, on coming back, is ocean's smile.

I've tried it under various aspects now
And never found its friendship fail,
But oft I've seen its power avail
To win a cheerful look from cloudiest brow.

I've tried in troublous times its joys to borrow,
And it has fanned me with its breeze,
Or finding me too hard to please
It spoke in storm and shamed me out of sorrow.

I've come to it again in times of joy,
And then its ripples seemed to speak,
And throw their kisses to my cheek,
As though it loved a gladsome heart t'employ.

In sickness I have sought its aid for healing,
When simply basking on its shore,
And seeming to desire no more,
I've learned towards it more than friendly feeling.

I've stood entranced by dear old ocean's side,
And thought of ages long since past;
Not one brief speck allowed to last,
And yet the ocean rolls with ceaseless tide.

Himself preparing by that ceaseless movement
This fair abode for Adam's race,
He then confined the ample space,
And left the ransomed earth for due improvement.

Then surely He the best can speak of man;
He's witnessed all our changes made;
The kingdoms' first foundation laid,
Their rise, their power, their fall in briefest span.

And thence His doom ; thus saith the Prince of Peace :
"Give back thy dead, thou mighty sea,
Ere thou art brought no more to be,
And then thy witness shall for ever cease.

"The earth's whole ages are within thy ken,
Thou know'st the mercies God has brought,
The follies that the world has wrought,
And thou wouldst witness 'gainst the sons of men."

"The sea to be no more," is then in love
A mercy promised to mankind,
Wherein our sinful race may find
The thoughts that in destruction our Heavenly Father move.

LXIV.

THIS TRIAL BEST.

THERE'S One who knoweth what is best,
That is enough for me ;
But yet my soul makes the request
That I that "best" may see.

Not mere submission to the Rod
Would I in suffering learn,
Nor see alone the Hand of God
In sorrow's each new turn.

His chastisements are good to know
  And precious when received,
High mounts the soul from things below
  When from the rod relieved.

But these are lessons far too small
  For my aspiring mind,
The present sorrow "best of all,"
  This would I ask to find.

Nor shall e'en this too forward prayer
  Be of the Lord denied,
Each deepest fountain of our care
  Is ever well supplied.

"Look out of self," methinks I hear
  The Great Physician say;
"Look to the Saviour ever near,
  Here is thy remedy."

One Best there is, One first of all
  The suffering ones among;
And sorrows, trials, "best" we call
  That to the Lord belong.

Endured for that bless'd Saviour's sake,
  And in His very name,
These are the things which ever make
  Our sorrow's highest claim.

To see them all in Christ my Lord
  A portion of His woe,
Myself just resting on His Word,
  And learning patience so:

To see the wounds inflicted now
  As lighting on His Head,
'Tis thus He bids us heal the blow,
  And souls be comforted.

Then is it not from this I learn
  The value of the thorn?
Its sharpest point to Him I turn
  By whom the Crown was worn.

Sure thus I learn how best to bear
  My trials as they come,
How best the glorious Crown to wear
  In the Eternal Home.

And thus, O Lord, thou dost in love
  Acknowledge my request,
Dost bid me lift my woes above
  In Christ to know them "best."

Hence, too, in sorrow each new thought
  On Christ my Lord shall rest,
Thus shall my longing soul be taught
  "This Trial is the Best."

LXV.

"I do set My bow in the cloud." (Gen. ix. 13.)

How bright does fancy paint that wondrous day
When, from the Ark set free, in brief array
There issued the new Masters of the earth,
A race rejoicing in its second birth!

Bright with the promise of a life secure,
As long as human ages should endure,
From deluge-desolation, how earth's frame
Swelled with its praise to the Creator's Name!

Shall thought imagine that a thunder-cloud
Swept o'er the scene of joy with echoes loud?
Recalling to the rescued ones the fear
That oft appalled them in their deluge-year?

If such their need, 'twas only that a word
Of Everlasting Promise from the Lord
Might comfort bring, and token might be given
Of love enduring ratified in Heaven.

"My Bow is in the Cloud," unseen, unknown
To mortal eye until the sun has shone;
Light cast upon the darkness, man shall see
The promise certain to Eternity.

Unfailing evidence of love unchanged!
No curse upon creation! All arranged
To lighten every burden that we bear,
To calm the soul, to moderate its fear.

"The Bow is in the Cloud," for every place
Where sorrow loves its deepest lines to trace,
For every time though desolate and dark,
For all that find their Refuge in the Ark.

Let but the Light arise, and every eye
May look upon the Cloud rejoicingly,
Man finding traces of his Saviour's ways
May span his sorrows as a source of praise.

The darkest cloud His presence most reveals,
To man most needing love the promise seals;
'Tis then 'mid storms and tempest roaring loud
I learn to seek the Bow upon the Cloud.

Bright token of the covenant displayed,
Thy colour on the cloud-bank softly laid,
Be to my life the evidence approved
That in my deepest sorrows I am loved.

"Bow in the Cloud," when death's chill hand I feel,
Do thou thy glories to my soul reveal,
And tell me of a Saviour's Light and Love
Embracing Earth below and Heaven above.

LXVI.

"Fashioned like unto His glorious body." (Phil. iii. 21.)

MORE like to Thee, Saviour, more like to Thee,
Chiefest of blessings well is it known to be,
Whate'er can compass this
Must bring a hope of bliss,
More like to Thee, Saviour, more like to Thee.

More like to Thee, Saviour, more like to Thee,
What if the blessing be drawn from adversity?
Welcome the trial sent
Even in punishment
If it can make us, Lord, more like to Thee.

More like to Thee, Saviour, more like to Thee?
Sure of the blessing, Lord, in an eternity;
Who would not longing pray
For the eternal day
When we shall rise, Saviour, like unto Thee?

More like to Thee, Saviour, more like to Thee,
Even this body, now weighed with infirmity,
Loves its bright hope to bear
Of the glad call to share
Blest Realms of Glory, Lord, like unto Thee.

More like to Thee, Saviour, more like to Thee,
Glorious Vision, oh! when shall it perfect be?
Haste, Lord, the coming hour
Of Thine Almighty power
When by Thy Grace we rise like unto Thee.

More like to Thee, Saviour, more like to Thee,
Waiting and watching-time, how long soe'er it be;
Make it, we pray Thee, blest
By a step daily pressed
On to perfection, Lord, like unto Thee.

More like to Thee, Saviour, more like to Thee,
In Thy forbearing love, kindness, and sympathy;
Wilt Thou not grace afford,
O Thou sustaining Lord,
Making us every hour more like to Thee?

More like to Thee, Saviour, more like to Thee,
Let all the world around Thine in our graces see,
We will in patience wait,
Blessed to anticipate
Joy in arising, Lord, like unto Thee.

LXVII.

"My beloved is Mine." (Song of Solomon ii. 16.)

GREAT the joy and rich in glory
  That at Jesus' *birth* began,
Angels tell to earth the story,
  "Peace on earth, good-will to Man."

Christ *baptized*, well-lost in wonder
  They, who banks of Jordan trod,
To see the Heavens part asunder,
  And to hear the voice of God.

Jesus *tempted*, loving boldness
  Gathers strength for trial's hour,
Fears no storm of desert coldness,
  Satan has been shorn of power.

Jesus *midst* the sick and dying,
  Oh! how heart doth linger there!
All His loving words applying
  To the wants of suff'rers here!

I seem in fancy's thought to meet Him,
  Going on His weary way,
Taught by wond'ring love to greet Him,
  And to follow if I may.

He my bright *Example* ever,
Should I not His follower be?
Naught from Him my soul shall sever,
Much less when He calleth me.

He my *Teacher*, all is taught me
That I need on earth to learn:
He my *Shepherd*, how He sought me
And then made me to return!

Sure the faith and full of blessing,
That from Jesus' *Cross* I bore;
There I stood, and sin confessing,
Burthens fell to rise no more.

Risen Saviour, how Thy breaking
Every bond of Death assures!
All the ties of earth forsaking
How Thy life my soul allures!

Thou art now in power *ascended*,
Longing heart well knows the place;
Heav'n, it speaks of sorrows ended,
And th' abundance of Thy grace.

At the Right Hand of the Father
Sure Thy pleading is for me,
Else I could not hope to gather
Joy so sweet in Misery.

Thou art now for me preparing
  Glorious Dwelling at Thy side,
Hence I banish all my fearing
  And in faith secure abide.

Blessed Saviour, Thou art ever
  All I seek and all I need;
Thou dost save, and Thou wilt never
  Break this weak and bruised reed.

Strong in Thy Eternal Power
  I will boldly lift my head,
Thou art mine for every hour,
  And my soul is comforted:

Thou art mine for every blessing
  All this weary life along,
This shall be my one confessing—
  "Christ is mine," my endless song.

LXVIII.

EARTH'S PRESENT WINTER.

WHENCE into being sprang this world of ours?
Was it not winter heretofore? Earth's powers
Seeming to angel's eye as though concealed,
Its life and action, as it were, congealed,
Till some warm influence called them into birth,
And into vigour forced a new regenerate earth?

Earth's future known, no chilling wintry blast
Shall o'er its glorious face a cloud-shade cast;
Eternal spring with its expanding force
Shall brightly manifest its living source,
Or everlasting summer gladly prove
The power that sustains it to be perfect love.

One winter then is gone; that chaos-scene,
Which in a past Eternity has been,
Well may be called a winter; not a ray
Of sunlight nourishing a hope of day;
Dull, cheerless, ray-less ages, yet the mould
Whence All-creative powers ere long should earth unfold.

Germ of all earthly life was perfect there,
For Hand of God was moving everywhere:
Each beauty clear to His All-seeing Eye,
Who puts His limit to infinity;
Let Him but speak, creative powers bring
O'er all that chaos-scene an universal *Spring.*

And who shall tell how gloriously bright
Earth shone when He proclaimed, "Let there be light?"
How started into being all the mass
From birth to fulness that is made to pass!
'Twas *Spring-time* perfect, while each new-formed age
For growth of fresh perfections was the fitting stage.

Then God beheld it, and "'Twas very good,"
For all creation in its order stood;
Age gave to age the key-note of its praise
As morn with even perfected the days;
Thus teeming earth unconsciously advanced
And glided into *Summer* with its powers enhanced.

Luxuriant Summer! How thy bosom swells
Each varied depth explored so plainly tells;
'Tis written on the stones by Hand unseen—
How vast, how glorious thy wealth has been;
The tenants of the world, a giant-race
Late brought to light, thy rich luxuriance trace.

Nor less from age to age each passing day
Owned and rejoiced in its Creator's sway,
Creation's work all perfect, there was naught
The loving purposes of God to thwart;
Its *Autumn* thus insensibly began,
And gently ripening formed a blest abode for man.

Man, in the image of his God arrayed,
The mighty plan of the Great King displayed,
A world created as a fitting throne
For man, for God-like man and him alone,
And earth, by work of ages once complete,
Made for the creature-man a home of blessing meet.

Say, had not Spring and Summer seasons wrought
Their beauteous changes? Had not Autumn brought
Rich harvest of its fruits, ere man was born,
The highest of its glories to adorn?
The seasons all their perfect course had run
From Chaos-winter to the Harvest-time begun.

And man should be the reaper, all his toil
To gather fruit from the productive soil;
No labour His while yet in innocence,
He shared the resting of Omnipotence;
His highest work, his happiest employ
To cull from a Creator's presence endless joy.

Yes, if to reap be angels' duty fit
And harvest of the world accomplish it,
To gather souls redeemed by Jesus' blood
Within the garners of His own abode,
Say, was not man angelically blest
In work appointed, and in Heav'nly Sabbath-rest?

And rich had been his reaping, but he fell;
How deeply, let the desolation tell
In every field of promise, or the blast
Of chill dark Winter o'er creation cast;
Dost ask, "How fallen?" Nature's self replies,
"See o'er the earth the curse, the blight on Paradise."

'Tis *Winter;* for behold how reaps he now,
'Tis by his labour and the sweat of brow;
No fruits spontaneous, no, nor blossoms spring,
But under curse the fields their riches bring;
Death rules triumphant, and 'tis Winter chill
When man, his course outrun, is captive to its will.

'Tis Winter; see how every pulse of life
Beats feebly, while the elements of strife
Grow into power. Does the smitten soul
Long for the Holy Spirit's glad control?
See how the clouds obscure the mental sky,
And storms opposing rise in their intensity.

'Tis Winter, for the mind of man betrays
Its chilling influence in a thousand ways;
Albeit formed and loving to progress,
And to perfection hastening to press,
Its vigour fails, its energies are cramped,
Its power too oft contracted, and its ardour damped.

Just as in Winter-season swells the flood,
While o'er the earth the thickening tempests brood,
Then madly bursts its fetters unrestrained
As glorying in the freedom it has gained;
So earth has had its Deluge, and displayed
The universal ruin Sin and Death have made.

True, there are gleams of sunlight o'er the scene,
And fields are smiling where the floods have been;
Days of delight and happiness there are,
Which thousands learn, and nations love, to share;
So in the Winter-season there are hours
When earth would seem constrained to use her highest powers.

Not all repulsive is the Winter's force,
E'en though of life it seems to check the source;
So in the Winter of the world we find
'Tis strength with weakness, life with death, combined:
Bright have the periods been, when all of earth
Seemed well prepared and destined for a second birth.

One period such, when covenant of grace
Threw beams of sunlight over nature's face;
Still more, when earth a special people saw
From bondage brought and taught by Heav'nly Law;
Yet brighter far when, on that solemn morn,
A Saviour, Christ the Lord, a Virgin's Son, was born.

Yea, more than Summer-glories these; their light
Enough to make the deepest darkness bright,
Did but the world accept the offered gift,
And man with gratitude his heart uplift;
But man would dwell in darkness, for the chill
Of Winter numbs his power, as Sin enthrals his will.

Some hearts there are that beat with love Divine,
As o'er them beams of light and glory shine;
E'en as in cold of winter there may grow,
Some flower rare, protected by the snow;
Just like the Snowdrop, some few hearts grow warm
'Mid wintry chills, and by their early beauty charm.

Were there no spirits upon earth to prove
How mists of Winter heaven-driven move,
Did all remain as though congealed with frost,
Were life in action only tempest-tossed,
Who could its sorrows bear, constrained to dwell
In world of light bereft, and thus akin to Hell?

But not so Mercy has arranged the sphere
Where man shall nourish faith or test his fear;
'Mid Winter's coldest blast a voice is heard
To comfort suffering hearts with loving word;
It bids him look from storms of earth away
To realms of nightless space, to light of endless day.

E'en in our deepest woe it seems to tell,
By God's appointment storms and tempests swell,
Naught is without its blessing, rightly seen,
All had its good whatever it has been,
Look to the coming of a brighter year
In which the Harvest's Lord has promised to appear.

The months of dreary Winter soon are past,
Earth's toils have no permission given to last,
Naught bears the impress of complete decay,
And dreariest night is but a step to day;
All, all some proof of hidden power bring,
That seeks its full expansion in Eternal Spring.

'Tis but a season then, this Winter-time,
Our present world its best-appointed clime;
Cease, cease, my soul to entertain a fear,
Still less for present sorrows drop the tear;
Look up, the gleams of light embrace the sky,
And all betokens that the warmth of Spring is nigh.

Go seek the dreariest sufferer of earth
And bid him catch some spark of holy mirth;
Sin shall be conquered, sorrow be no more,
Life shall expand where Death has reigned before;
Earth with its new-born energies shall rise
And form for Christ a Throne, for Man a Paradise.

LXIX.

"RING THE OLD YEAR OUT."

RING, ring the Old Year out,
  Make it a merry sound,
Banish all fears and doubt,
  Ere new ones come around;
Time is a tyrant-lord
  Our life's wealth amassing,
We then can well afford
  To welcome its passing.

Ring, ring the Old Year gone
  With all its sorrowing,
Let it stand all alone,
  Naught elsewhere borrowing;
Record it has of grief,
  No need enlarging it,
Seek not to gain relief
  By overcharging it.

Ring, ring the Old Year passed,
  Ne'er to come back again,
Were it to be our last
  Who would e'en then complain?
Rather in this be glad,
  Years have their end secured,
Things that make spirit sad
  Briefly must be endured.

Ring, ring the Old Year's end,
  Gone are its hopes and joy,
E'en though it be a friend
  Thanks should the tongue employ;
Ne'er would we see its face
  Once gone and for ever,
Happy the time and place
  Such friendships dissever.

Ring, ring the Old Year out,
  Mercies and blessings flown,
No fears nor trembling doubt
  Harass the faithful one:
Years are the measuring
  Life's feeble span awhile,
Life is but treasuring
  God's own eternal smile.

Ring, ring the Old Year out,
That smile its best feature,
Ne'er can it be without
Its hope for each creature;
God's love in Christ the Son
Knows no diminishing,
Bright are its hopes begun,
Brighter their finishing.

Ring then, the Old Year passed,
Hearts should be lighter far,
Home that for aye will last
Shines with a brighter star;
Years as they pass along
Tell us of joys to come,
Bidding us learn the song
Of our Eternal Home.

FLORENCE, *December* 31*st*, 1861.

LXX.

"RING THE NEW YEAR IN."

RING, aye ring the New Year in,
Welcome to the stranger give,
Fitting 'tis thus to begin
Each new period we live:

Whatsoever it may be,
  Day of light or day of gloom,
Where there is uncertainty
  For a welcome there is room.

Sailor standing on the shore
  Looks upon the swelling main,
Thinks he of his home no more
  Longing for the sea again:
Bids he then his friends adieu
  Cheerily and light in heart,
One chief object in his view
  How and when he may depart.

Is there nothing in the thought
  Such should be the Christian's aim?
In a higher service taught
  Sure his love should be the same;
"Onwards, forwards," is his cry,
  Higher steps than heretofore,
These to reach, with eager eye
  He surveys the Heav'nly shore.

Stand, and look then well to-day,
  'Tis for thought a resting-place;
Scan awhile the Heav'nward way,
  Christian heart, enriched by Grace;

And if Mercy still has spared
  This new period to begin,
Thinking of what may be shared,
  Ring, oh! ring the New Year in.

Grant that life is mostly toil,
  Earth for man a weary scene,
Future blessings will not spoil
  Any gladness that has been;
Rather would their prospect cheer
  Did they fully play their part,
Hear them speak with accent clear
  'Twere a joy to dullest heart.

What if sorrows cast before
  Chill the ardour of the soul?
Gleams of light as seen the more
  Should all doubts and fears control;
Let the world be hurrying on
  To its end of ripening woe,
'Tis but an appointed doom,
  He who saves will have it so.

Let the sky be overcast,
  Darkness near, and clouds afar,
Let the troubled nations haste
  To the deadly strife of war;

Hope there is of a release
  From all labours, pain, and care,
He who is the Prince of Peace
  Reigns supreme and everywhere.

Ring, then, ring the New Year in,
  All our future is secure,
All our work the Crown to win,
  And the strength for it is sure;
Years roll by and quickly bring
  Trusting hearts towards their home,
Then what aids th' accomplishing
  Surely as a good must come.

Fears be hushed, ye doubts give way,
  Satan's struggles are in vain,
All is pressing to the day
  When our King shall come to reign;
Be it far, or be it near,
  Let its hope our life engage,
None can justify a fear
  In our christian pilgrimage.

Pilgrims, raise aloft the eye,
  See the sky with glory filled,
Jesus in His Majesty,
  Man exalted, nations stilled;

Each new period seems to say—
"Soon will cease the scourge of Sin,
Welcome the approach of day,
Ring then, ring the New Year in."

FLORENCE, *January* 1, 1862.

LXXI.

THE CIRCUMCISION OF CHRIST.

WHAT strange compassion! Love beyond our thought,
Salvation by Immanuel's suff'ring bought!
The Lord against His own Beloved One
That rebel man might e'en become a Son!
"God" thus "for us," Himself must humbled be,
Must share each portion of humanity,
Must know of flesh some struggles that are vain,
And learn obedience by the body's pain.
Hence cries of helpless infancy, the bands
Of childhood needed at a mother's hands,
The mark of outward covenant, the pledge
Of highest spiritual privilege:
A name must be recorded, though 'twere given
Long since by loving Messenger from Heaven,

"Jesus," the name that every tongue shall bless,
And yet fulfilment of earth's righteousness:
He that should "save His people from their sin"
Must e'en a life of suffering begin:
O! say what miracle of love is this
That life protracted for His people's bliss!
Mounts not the pulse of every Christian heart
With Jesus' suffering to bear a part?
Vain thought, O man of tenderest sympathy,
This is the very work of Deity—
Thine is to look believing, and to love,
Then seek the circumcision from Above;
The spirit's work to mortify thy lust;
Cut off the sin-badge of a world accurst,
Lay bare the inmost soul to each appeal
Of conscience, and the wounds of Satan heal,
Obedient to the law of God, and live
Thy growth from Christ as loving to derive—
True day of circumcision that declares
The grace that sinner with the Saviour shares!
Mine be it now to tread this suffering way,
And thus to keep a living Holy-day!

FLORENCE, 1862.

LXXII.

THE EPIPHANY.

"Thy light is come, arise and shine,"
Thus spake the prophet to the sons of Israel,
Nor less the Gospel with its news Divine
Would speed on earth the advent of Immanuel:
Ye shepherds, freely tell
How, in your watches of the night,
Angelic praises swell;
And how, rejoicing in the light,
Ye haste, if haply ye may see
The early rising of your King's Epiphany.

What though the son of Beor's trance
To watch with eager eyes, the Eastern sages led,
Lest some new-risen star unseen perchance
Might show the vision of the King accomplished?
Shall Jacob's star appear
And throw no gleam of light abroad?
It rises bright and clear,
Its radiance hastening to afford
New light to every watching eye
That patient looks and waits for the Epiphany.

See where some gleam is shot afar,
The distant nations hail the long expected sign;
The Royal Sages guided by the star
Haste their appointed search whence all true glories shine;
Nor shall ye, Princes, fail,
Your patient watching soon shall cease,
In hope the King to hail
Ye shall embrace the Prince of Peace;
Then tell, as long as life may be,
The worship and the joy of His Epiphany.

The Prince of Peace is manifest,
No earthly palace there to mar the lowly scene,
The King of all the Nations stands confessed
In dwelling humblest that could e'er on earth have been:
Oh! tell how pride of man
Hence gathers all its true reproof,
Bid earth-born Princes scan
The Virgin Mother's lowly roof,
Then cast their look of faith on high,
And learn abasement from their King's Epiphany.

Nor have ye less your songs to raise
For hearts' permitted welcome given to the King,
The richest offerings of adoring praise
So well-betokened by the royal gifts ye bring:

By these the world is taught
What earthly gifts of treasure best
By sinners may be brought
To Jesus the Atoning Priest;
From your glad offerings we see
The due return from Man for the Epiphany.

For let its ligh on men once shine,
Encircling, as it did a great blasphemer's head,
The sinner yielding to the Power Divine
Henceforth by hand unseen petitions to be led;
Untaught to watch and wait
As your glad guidance seems to teach,
Yet, by a love as great,
Your power to worship he may reach,
Permitted by that love to be,
Though late, a sharer in the King's Epiphany.

Come then, ye people, Gentile, Jew,
All nations of whatever character and age,
This blessed season has its truth for you,
And should each willing heart's profoundest zeal engage;
The long-expecting Seer,
The Sage of Philosophic Lore,
Souls learning to revere,
Or long instructed to adore,
All meet in blessed company
To welcome a return of the Epiphany.

Let then the light arise and shine,
There's naught of earth so dark but may admit a ray,
Once let the soul be pierced by Power Divine
The Lord will manifested be in perfect day:
Who thence shall love so well?
Who know so fully joys above?
Not eastern sage could tell
Such triumphs of a Saviour's love:
Let him this day triumphant be,
And He will freely make His own Epiphany.

FLORENCE, 1862.

LXXIII.

"The angel of the Lord encampeth round about them that fear Him, and delivereth them." (Psalm xxxiv. 7.)

FATHER, a promise in Thy Word I've found,
The angel of the Lord encampeth round
The souls that fear Him, and delivereth:"
Then 'tis a holy, filial, contrite fear,
That makes the children of Thy love to share
The presence of the Aid that comforteth.

And yet methinks the history of the past
Tells of the light *that* Presence has o'ercast
  On many a soul whose only thought was dread,
When trust has failed and faith o'erpowered been,
And only terror triumphed o'er the scene,
  Thine angel came to man and comforted.

True, they were subjects, servants, sons of Thine,
On whom that light has been allowed to shine,
  And none but trusting hearts the blessing share;
Nor would we think a coward fear to be
For Thy deliv'rance th' admitted plea,
  And yet such hope Thy Mercy bids us dare.

'Twas when the Patriarch, banished from his home,
With nought to cheer him for the time to come,
  By journey wearied, laid him down to sleep,
A glorious vision passed before his eyes,
There came, there rose, angelic companies,
  A holy watch o'er earth designed to keep.

Years passed of blessing, full of wealth his hand,
Again he seeks his long-left fatherland,
  But shall a brother's wrath forgotten be?
Let conscience answer, "Well may Jacob fear;"
And then let God reply, "There shall appear
  "Two hosts of angels to deliver thee."

The Angel of His Presence! who shall tell
What strength the Patriarch gained at Peniel?
  "I will not let thee go unless Thou bless;"
Hear him thus speak, and let not coward heart
Henceforth from battle or from burthen start,
  Angelic aid instructed to confess.

Who, think we, knew the blessed truth so well
As He, the Lawgiver of Israel,
  The Angel's presence in the fire revealed?
Strange should his lips the constant theme refuse,
Or heart the gladd'ning recollection lose
  Of truth by mercies so transcendant sealed.

Yea, 'tis a nation's voice that shall proclaim
Their Lord and King's imperishable Name,
  "The Angel of His presence," sent to save;
Or, if the tongue of Israel be mute,
Assyria's slaughtered host shall ne'er dispute
  The awful ministration Angels have.

Proof higher yet, when proudest Eastern-king
Commands his foolish idol-worshipping,
  And hottest furnace claims the martyrs bound,
An angel to the monarch's eye appears,
The glorious form of Son of God He wears,
  And captives, angel-freed, unscathed are found.

A wondrous evidence of Truth confessed!
How does it bid the soul in faith to rest
  Upon the arm of an Omnipotence!
How yearns the heart to glorify the aid
Which Power Almighty to the Angels bade,
  The Spirits minis'tring in Man's defence!

Or shall a suffering soul be found on earth
'Mid sons that fear and know such feeling's worth?
  How blessed of Angel's guardianship to speak!
Still more to plead, in prophet's faith and word
That friend may see the Armies of the Lord,
  Prepared his sure deliverance to seek!

An Angel-Camp! The very mountains fill
In sight of man by the Great Captain's will
  With horsemen and with chariots of fire.
Look up and trust, all ye the Lord who fear,
When foes are highest, there shall soon appear
  For your defence a Succour that is higher.

LXXIV.

THE CURE.

WHY should a *Soul* redeemed refuse
  Its grateful song to raise?
Shall storm of trial plead excuse
  For negligence of praise?

Why hangs the *Harp* upon the trees
  Untouched by Christian Hand?
Shall coward heart's infirmities
  Its indolence demand?

The *Lips*, why silent? Once employed
  To sing a Saviour's Love?
Can tongue that such a praise enjoyed
  Forget with joy to move?

The *Hands*, so feeble! that once swept
  The living chords along,
What wintry coldness can have crept,
  The Christian souls among?

'Tis Grace that's needed, Heav'nly Grace,
  To strike some chord within,
A light from the Redeemer's face
  Upon the soul to shine:

Its source, I trace it all along,
  In Heaven, I know it there;
If not an echo of our song,
  An answer to our prayer.

Thou, Lord of Grace, my *Soul* must take
  Within Thy gracious fold,
And Thou its every thought shalt make
  For all Thy service bold.

My *Harp*, within Thy hands I place
  So long on willows hung,
And Thou wilt tune it by Thy Grace,
  Though broken and unstrung.

My *Lips* I dedicate to Thee,
  To whom their praise belongs,
And Thou their very life wilt be,
  The source of all their songs.

My *Hands* shall evermore be Thine
  By Thy direction taught;
Soul, *Harp*, and *Lips*, and *Hands* combine
  To praise Thee as they ought.

LXXV.

"Unto you it is given in the behalf of Christ, not only to believe on Him, but also to suffer for His sake." (Phil. i. 29.)

'Tis e'en as Faith, of gifts the best,
Which, grasping highest things of Heaven,
And needed most, as all attest,
Is freely, plentifully, given:

As Faith, just so to "Suffer truly,"
Itself is gift from Heav'n supplied,
A precious gift acknowledged duly
With reference to the Crucified.

"In Christ's behalf," for so 'tis worded,
And then to "suffer for His sake,"
'Tis thus the gift is now accorded,
'Tis these the giving precious make.

And truly could the thousand blessings
Of Christlike suffering be seen,
Unceasing would be our caressings
Of the dear Hand that smites, I ween.

Mount up then to the Higher Station,
All ye who doubt the trouble's aim,
Admit within the contemplation
On each of us the Saviour's claim;

Shall there be sufferings yet to lighten
  A sinner's pathway to His Home?
Yea, surely 'tis a thought to brighten
  The darkest shadow of the tomb:

Can I do aught for Christ my King?
  Is there one thing of His remains
That I can aid accomplishing
  E'en through the soul's or body's pains?

How gladly would I offered be
  On such an altar of my Lord!
Naught but an honour could I see
  My very life-blood to afford.

His purposes can never fail,
  He has some blessed end in view,
His love, His mercy will avail
  My work for Him to make me do.

Suffice it for my loving heart
  By Him each suffering is given,
I bear with Him some lowly part
  Of toil on earth, of joy in Heaven.

LXXVI.

"Abide with us: for it is toward evening." (Luke xxiv. 29.)

Far spent the day, its varied glories fail,
  How soon will shades of night its beauty hide!
But e'en the darkest moment I can hail
  If Thou, O Saviour, wilt with me *Abide.*

So with life's evening drawing to a close,
  Its waves roll on with a resistless tide;
But not a fear disturbs my calm repose,
  For Thou, O Saviour, dost with me *Abide.*

Its pleasures, they are passed, its friendships o'er,
  Yet every thought of loss I put aside,
Joys Thou suppliest holier and more,
  Since Thou, O Saviour, dost with me *Abide.*

Securely kept my soul in perfect peace,
  I see the door of Mercy opened wide,
For Thou didst give me from my sins release,
  When Thou with me consented'st to *Abide.*

Should I not welcome the approach of Death,
  And gladly watch its unresisted stride?
I can look up, and calmly yield my breath,
  For Thou, O Saviour, wilt with me *Abide.*

I know Thy mercy and Thy promise sure,
  I've learned in Thy protection to confide,
Thy love and patience cannot but endure,
  Thyself with sinners deigning to *Abide.*

Yet, Lord, *Abide* with me; I cannot live,
  Unless Thy Hand is ever at my side;
I cannot die, or spirit freely give,
  If Thou, O Lord, dost not with me *Abide.*

The day far spent; though night is given by Thee,
  My soul in hours of darkness Thou must hide;
Then call me near Thee, by Thy Throne to be,
  By Thee I live, and one with Thee *Abide.*

LXXVII.

"In all points tempted like as we are." (Heb. iv. 15.)

My Saviour tempted! can it be
Such trial was endured for me?
How should not every soul-pulse bless
The pathway of the Wilderness?
      Nor thanks alone
      My due I own,
      To Christ I turn
      That I may learn
The healing of my soul's distress.

See what His answer when the plea
Was urged of His Humanity;
"These stones command that they be bread,
Let hunger from Thy God be fed;"
"The soul ne'er lives
By bread He gives,
The living Word
Is from the Lord
A feast for loving servants spread."

Nor baffled is the Tempter, he
Can make such food a snare to be;
"Thou'rt raised to pinnacle of earth,
Then prove the declaration's worth;
The angels' hand
At Thy command
Shall keep Thy feet,
Thine aid complete,
Test by Thy fall Thy Heavenly birth!"

What! shall we tempt the Lord, and see
The proof of our temerity?
"Thou shalt not thus the promise try,
And then expect the succour nigh;
Enough thine aid,
Each step is laid,
One glance astray
Beyond thy way,
He will not grace nor aid supply."

And shall not Satan vanquished flee
And own the Conqueror's victory?
Nay, "worship me," the Tempter cries,
"I'll give thee what around thee lies;
"Thy wearied knee
Bow down to me,
And I will make
The world partake
Full knowledge of thy Masteries."

The pride of life, the lust of eye,
The world, he gives it all to me,
What then the refuge of my soul?
"Behind me, Satan, Tempter foul,
'Tis rank offence
Thy vain pretence,
To God alone
Thy service own,
Thy heart, thy life, He asks the whole."

Bless'd Saviour! Thou wert tried for me
That I might know Thy constancy,
For me the Tempter was defied
That I with grace might be supplied;
The trial sped,
And Satan fled;
The triumph Thine,
'Tis ever mine,
For naught to faith can be denied.

Fight on, thou tempted, it shall be
A step to angel's ministry,
Thy weapons from the Conquering Lord,
Thy vict'ry by the Written Word,
In every part
Thy troubled heart
May find its peace
And wondrous grace,
Behold thine aid, the Spirit's sword.

LXXVIII.

"Thou knowest that I love thee." (John xxi. 15.)

Thy loving kindness, gracious Lord, demands
A willing heartfelt service at my hands,
Why then must all my life reveal
The poverty of praise I feel?
So coldly, heartlessly, I serve,
So sadly feeble every nerve,
My very service tongue shall scarcely tell,
And yet Thou knowest that I love Thee *well.*

Times there have been when unexpected sin
Has seemed to gain a mastery within,
What then of will to serve Thee, Lord?
Poor evidence can I afford

Of ought the stamp of love that bears:
Were judgments passed by what appears
I could not breathe confession thus to men,
But yet Thou knowest that I loved Thee *then.*

Heart has awhile seemed clasped in the embrace
Of earthly objects, honour, power, praise;
Where then the pulse of Love to beat
That casts its crowns before Thy feet,
That from Thy blessed service claims
Its highest joy, its purest aims?
My cold affections I would fain deplore,
And yet Thou knowest that I love Thee *more.*

A bitter constrast there has sometimes been
Thy perfect and my faulty will between;
E'en conscience self must own
A harvest of rebellion sown,
Self-love, self-interest at best
Too often into action pressed;
No higher impulse can I dare to boast,
And yet Thou knowest that I love Thee *most.*

So too in very worship gladly paid
When all my worldly thoughts awhile seem
stayed,
Some folly or distracting care
Has claimed my heart's regard to share;

Where, where the love t'enwrap the soul
Within its unrestrained control?
Howe'er I strive, the spirit is unruly,
And yet Thou knowest that I love Thee *truly*.

Yea, Thine my love by Thine own gracious planting,
Wilt Thou not pardon then whate'er is wanting?
I dare not doubt Thy loving hand
Howe'er I fail of Thy demand;
Thy love in Christ must perfect be,
Creating thoughts o love in me:
Nor will I fear that aught the bond can sever,
Because Thou knowest I will love Thee *ever*.

LXXIX.

"Lord, I believe; help Thou mine unbelief." (Mark ix. 24.)

A Father pleading for his son,
That son of Satan led, and dumb,
How plain to every eye the sorrows of our race
Man may to fellow-man complain,
But human aid is sought in vain,
For cure and sympathy there is one only Place.

Thus learn we from the touching scene,
When Jesus had transfigured been,
That, coming to his friends, had met his wond'ring sight;
"Lord, if Thou canst," the father cries,
"Do aught to heal our miseries,
On us, O Lord, have mercy, show Thy healing might."

And will He deign to give reply!
When failed His loving sympathy?
"If thou canst only trust, full sure is thy relief."
Oh! with what energy of trust,
That parent, humbled to the very dust,
"Lord, I believe," exclaims; "help Thou mine unbelief."

Nor needs the gracious Lord of power
One word from sufferer the more,
Enough that parent's humble trust and lowly faith;
No more Satanic power of ill
That child leads captive at his will,
The Lord of Life hath spoken, and He conquers Death.

And has not such a scene a tongue,
Ten thousand works of love among,
That tells of sorrow's healing from the gracious Lord?
The need as great as heretofore,
No less our sorrows Jesus bore,
And hence He utters still that same heart-searching word.

Thou sorrowing, suffering, sin-tossed soul,
Just simply comprehend the whole,
There's naught impossible to a believing mind;
Though into deepest waters cast,
Though caught by fiery furnace blast,
If only thou wilt trust, deliverance thou wilt find.

Whate'er the suffering, the tear,
Of body or of mind the care,
Whether from ills of self, of children, or of home,
Take them to Jesus for their cure,
His healing mercies still endure,
And He can raise the dead ones from the lowest tomb.

One only plea restrains His hand,
Obedience to His own command,
"Believe that I will give thee the desired relief;"
He waits from sufferer to hear
To that command the answer clear,
"Oh Lord, I do believe, help thou mine unbelief."

Yea, and such language would I learn
In trial's every varied turn,
Wherein before the Lord to pour my deepest grief;
When suff'ring from the heaviest ill,
By folly caused or Satan's skill,
"Lord, I believe," I'll cry, "help Thou mine unbelief."

LXXX.

ASH WEDNESDAY.

HUSHED are the sounds of semi-heathen revelry
That day by day have broken on the ear;
Strange that the mixing mirth grotesque and devilry
Should mark a portion of the Christian year!
But pandering to the passions base
That tide o'er our afflicted race
Is rightly deemed too natural to all,
And this the groundwork of a Christian Carnival.

Nor scarcely less mysterious th' appointed fast
That bids each sound of merriment to cease,
'Twould seem that Jewish bondage had been doomed to last,
And Christians are denied their full release;
But let the contrast prove in part
The alternate surgings of the heart,
Now wild with ecstacy beyond control,
Now cast to very depths by th' afflictings of the soul.

O strange perversion! How should constant thanks be ours
For freedom from this double bond enjoyed,
Nor let us e'er forget that all our mental powers
In simple worship may be best employed;
Each longing of the purest thought,
Each need of ours by suffering taught
May find its access to the Throne of Grace,
And catch some gleam of comfort from th' Saviour's face.

True penitential feeling surely must demand
The lowliest homage that the lips can pay,
No earnest spirit of repentance can have planned
The Saturnalia of holiday;
But let not Christian heart forget
There may be foolishness as great;
The fast that God requires is one of love,
When heart and soul to energetic action move.

And such our season in its aspirations clear,
Its spring the feeling of true penitence,
Souls, humbled to the dust, to Throne of Grace draw near,
Their sin's confession not a vain pretence;
"True contrite hearts," their prayer, "Create,
Have pity, Lord, on our estate,
'Tis Mercy that we ask, our sins forgive,
Henceforth for others good and to Thy praise we live."

FLORENCE, 1862.

LXXXI.

"Speak unto the children of Israel, that they go forward." (Exod. xiv. 15.)

GOD'S work complete! Then mark the way He leads,
See how the chosen flock the Shepherd feeds;
By Him delivered, they shall still depend
On Him as Guide and Keeper to the end;
Their fetters burst, oh! let the people haste
Their Homeward journey, till all foes be past.

"Haste for thy life;" unceasingly believe
That thy escape from bonds is not to live;
'Tis life's beginning, 'tis the blossom burst,
The flower of beauty into vigour thrust;
But life is action, contest, struggle, toil,
Beware how quickly storm will flower spoil.

And sons are soon in danger; yea, a cry
Is heard ere yet their guidance they can try,
Before them, waters of the pathless sea,
Behind them, wrath of injured enemy:
Say, shall the image of a God of Love
Be seen o'er those tumultuous waves to move?

Hear what the voice of human faith will say,
"Fear not, be still, behold Salvation's way;
Peace, fainting hearts, ye troubled spirits, peace;
The Lord shall fight for you and bring release."
Exalted faith, the triumph of a mind
That loves its courage in the Lord to find!

Yet not the teaching that our God would give,
Nor fugitive from wrath should best receive;
'Tis faith of action which the Lord desires,
The fight of faith our very life requires;
"Why criest thou?" the question of His love,
"Command My people that they forward move."

What, shall the Host of Israel tempt the waves?
Or is it thus the God of Battle saves?
Escape denied, naught is there but one way,
And that a passage opened through the sea;
But what the wave or tempest to the Lord,
Who formed the worlds by His creative word?

Reflection of His Image, 'tis the path
Whereby His people He will save from wrath;
An emblem of His heart, unclosed to those
Who trust His aid, but firmly shut to foes:
See how the path for Israel expands,
How walls of water close to Egypt's bands!

Then let His people forward, onward go,
Let step be sure e'en though it may be slow;
No halting for the Christian, he must press
Through fire, and wave, and barren wilderness;
Each fitted best by Him who guides His sons,
No danger pathless for His chosen ones.

Think not, O man from Egypt's bondage freed,
Thy soul of Passive Faith alone has need;
One moment's glance to Heaven, if you will,
To calm the doubting spirit and be still;
Look for Almighty succour in the fight,
But only lent to stimulate thy might.

Press forward, Christian, speed thy glorious way,
Toil on, fight boldly, every fear allay;
No bondage further, there is fire by night
To guide thy steps, by day a perfect Light;
Thy Wilderness, the path that Jesus trod,
Conducts thee safely to thy Home, to God.

LXXXII.

"To me to live is Christ, and to die is gain." (Phil. i. 21.)

All gain, no loss,
Welcome the Cross,
Christ is present and has borne;
Why then should any Christian fear
The greatest suffering to bear,
Jesus sharing all the scorn?

All gain, no loss,
Even the Cross,
From the Lord a special gift;
Who then that loves Him but receives
With gratitude whate'er He gives,
Heart to Him well-taught to lift?

No loss, all gain,
Naught is in vain,
Christ has brought us Death to Sin;
Full bless'd the death to things of sense,
The work of His Omnipotence
Gives us all in Christ to win

No loss, all gain,
Who shall complain?
Christ our Life and Righteousness;
He supplying, what can fail us?
He defending, who assail us?
Ever near to guard and bless?

All gain, no loss,
Light from the Cross
  Christ is shedding o'er our way;
    In Him we live, in Him we die,
    Christ is of Life the full supply,
  Guide to the Eternal Day.

No loss, all gain,
Death shall explain
  Every doubt and mystery,
    How all came from Jesus' giving,
    Whence the secret of our living,
  Love the simple history.

No loss, all gain,
Who shall refrain
  Death's approach from welcoming?
    Tempter banished, storms expended,
    Jesus' presence, sorrows ended,
  This is Life with Heaven's King.

LXXXIII.

"I reckon that the sufferings of this present time are not worthy to be compared with the glory which shall be revealed in us." (Rom. viii. 18.)

HEAR thus a sufferer speak, let no one dare,
Though cheering it may seem,
His darkest cloud of suffering compare
With Heaven's faintest gleam;
The Hand of Man can hold no balance true,
Nor thought conceive the make-weight that is due.

Who shall his sorrows, howsoe'er intense,
Beside His Glory place?
Or single claim to honour make pretence
From trial's path to trace?
Unworthy these to fill one thought of man,
Whene'er in Faith he strives his Home to scan.

As pales the starlight in the early dawn
And moon scarce seems to shine,
So thought of past dejection is withdrawn
Beyond the vision's line
Whene'er the glories of the Future rise
To wake within the soul their harmonies.

Nay, trace the sorrow to its proper source,
  See trial in its bloom,
Or mark the suff'rer span his life-long course
  In prospect of his Home;
    Shall he deem worthy of a glorious crown
    A work or toil he ne'er can call his own?

Stained is each Christian's holiest act with sin,
  Defiled is every Saint,
'Tis Grace continues, as it must begin,
  To remedy the taint;
    In face of Glory then no sufferer dare
    His own poor feeble strength with Grace compare.

Or would the strengthened heart its reck'ning make?
  Just fathom Mercy's fount;
One glance at the Redeemer's sorrows take,
  'Twill aid the Soul's account;
    With Christ we suffer, and with Him we reign;
    None of himself henceforth will speak again.

Much less compare the Crown with Sorrow's Cross,
  The Glory with the Shame,
The future Gain with present heaviest Loss,
  The Praises with the Blame;
    The future, Christ's and it will ever bear
    A Glory and a Grace beyond compare.

LXXXIV.

"The inhabitant shall not say, I am sick." (Isaiah xxxiii. 24.)

Oh! for Heaven's glory hasting!
  Satan ne'er beguiling there,
Sorrow shades of gloom ne'er casting,
  Sickness ne'er begetting fear.

Great the blessing in affliction,
  Let not sufferer this deny,
But it rises from conviction
  Of its heav'enward tendency.

'Tis to make the Kingdom precious,
  Freed from sin and every stain;
'Tis to show the Saviour gracious
  In His own, His people's pain.

None shall tell of aught oppressing
  Through a glad Eternity,
What is sorrowful, distressing,
  Cannot in the Kingdom be.

Perfect body, dross forsaking,
  Like to Jesus glorified,
When in His glad likeness waking,
  I shall then be satisfied.

No more fears of loved ones failing;
  One and spotless is the Bride;
No suspense nor doubt assailing,
  Languor, weakness cast aside.

No more doubt, its traces vanish,
  Life eternal filling all;
Light and life for ever banish
  Every remnant of the fall.

Oh! for faith and courage stronger!
  Jesus standeth at the door;
Bear our pains few moments longer,
  Soon they cease to vex no more.

LXXXV.

"More than conquerors." (Rom. viii. 37.)

GLAD the Warrior, battle ended,
  Victory gained and peace secured,
Triumphs of his King extended,
  End for toil to be endured;
    Sheath thy sword, Victorious Warrior,
  Well has it thy Rest procured.

Proud the Wrestler, struggle over,
Every foeman prostrate laid,
Laurels fit his temples cover,
All his labours well repaid;
Closed thy toil, Victorious Wrestler,
Thou mayst proudly lift thy head.

Less shall Christian, sin defeated,
Song of triumph gladly raise,
Contest finished, oft repeated,
Bitter toil of many days?
Work complete, Victorious Christian,
Look for thy Eternal Praise.

Sorer struggles, contest longer,
Thy endurance better prove;
Satan strong, but thou art stronger
By the aid of Heavenly Love;
Bow the head, Victorious Soldier,
All thy power from Above.

Earthly triumphs well accorded
Mark the Warrior's world-wide fame,
Wrestler's victory well rewarded
Gives to him 'mongst men a name;
Thine is nobler, Christian Victor,
Greater toil bears higher claim.

"More than Conqueror," thus exalted
Every Christian victor's place,
Sacrifice by Jesus salted
Well attests the powers of grace;
Thou wilt own it, called to Glory,
When thou seest face to face.

Grace abounding, how it raises
All the issues of our fight!
Limiting the Christian's praises
To the sources of his might:
"More than Conqueror," thus declaring
Good the self-abasing sight.

"More than Conqueror." Contest's blessing
In its due improvement lies,
Trial of our faith confessing,
See it in its exercise;
Need so urgent, Struggling Soldier,
How thy heart-felt prayers arise!

"More than Conqueror," Battle raging,
Angel forms are watching there,
Contest hosts of Heav'n engaging,
Man their triumph comes to share;
Learn from this, O Christian Soldier,
Higher, nobler, things to dare.

"More than Conqueror." Struggle ended,
Triumph warrior never knew
Greets the victor now ascended
With the glory that is due:
See the honours, Conquering Hero,
Christ Himself prepares for you.

Oh! for Grace to battle truly
'Gainst the foes of Christ my King;
I'll His praise acknowledge duly,
Yea, make courts of Heav'n to ring:
Owning His the Grace, the Conquest,
"More than Conqueror," I'll sing.

LXXXVI.

"And so shall we ever be with the Lord." (1 Thess. iv. 17.)

"*Be ever with the Lord.*"—Eternity!
The home, the life, the joy that is to be!
Our struggles over, and our labours done,
The course accomplished and the victory won,
The summons issued, and the angel-hand
Has safely guided to the promised land;
While thousand voices echo forth the Word,
"And so shall we be ever with the Lord."

"Be ever *with the Lord,*" to see His face
For ever beaming with surpassing grace;
To hear His welcome, as we near His Throne,
And cast before His feet our purchased crown;
To join with rapture th' unnumbered throng,
And chant the Lamb's and Moses' kindred song:
So great the blessings centred in the Word,
"And so shall we be ever with the Lord."

"*We* ever with the Lord," a mutual joy,
Unbroken adoration its employ!
Communion upon earth so blessed and sweet,
How glorious there when perfected we meet!
One Church, one Body, one Elected Bride
For ever by the Well-Beloved's side;
The joy eternal resting on the Word,
"And so shall we be ever with the Lord."

"*We* ever with the Lord," Apostles, Saints,
How wond'ring fancy the blest union paints!
The Martyr-hosts through tribulation come,
The Travellers o'er Wilderness at Home,
The Sin-bound freed, the weary ones at rest,
The toiling, sorrowing, together blest;
One band triumphant, glorying in the Word,
"And so shall we be ever with the Lord."

"*We* ever with the Lord," our Fathers there,
The loved ones taught so long on earth to share
Our joys and sorrows, weaknesses and might,
The dear supporters of our sinking fight,
The friends that warned of folly's devious path
Or snatched the falling from impending wrath;
No voice discordant, taught to speak the Word,
"And so shall we be ever with the Lord."

"*We* ever with the Lord:" Hast looked above,
Bereaved and sorrowing one, for her you love?
Afflicted mother, know thy child among
The spotless, innocent, the chief-loved throng—
Yea, brother, sister, left to walk alone,
The lost is but awhile before thee gone;
We meet to part no more, so runs the Word,
"And so shall we be ever with the Lord."

"Be *ever* with the Lord," Eternal Home
For coming ages, yet and yet to come!
O wonderful eternity, thy span
Beyond the thought of best-instructed man,
Without cessation, time, or end, or place,
As boundless as the exercise of Grace;
Enough for faith the promise of the Word,
"And so shall we be ever with the Lord."

"*Be ever with the Lord*," I want no more
Than cast a glance of patience to the shore;
One look of Faith, O give me, Lord, to Thee,
And though in trouble, I'll contented be,
Leave all that may concern my glory's day
To Him, who waits to wipe all tears away;
One truth sufficient, gathered from the Word,
"And so shall we be ever with the Lord."

LXXXVII.

"Ye are not as yet come to the Rest, and to the Inheritance which the Lord your God giveth you." (Deut. xii. 9.)

HIGHER, weary Traveller, higher,
This is not your place of Rest,
For, measured by your own desire,
Scant and poor it seems at best;
Its stains of sin no cloud can hide,
Ne'er would thy soul be satisfied
With such a place of Rest.

Yonder, weary Traveller, yonder
Is the place of Heavenly Rest;
Wilt thou never cease to wonder
That in this you are distressed?
The sorrows that bedew thine eye
Have their appointed ministry
To make thee see thy Rest.

Onward, weary traveller, onward
  Pressing to Thy promised Rest;
Struggling, see the Martyr-foreguard
  Raising their triumphal crest;
    There's not a Christian Victory
    That does not plainly tell to thee
      Through Struggle is thy Rest.

Nearer, weary Traveller, nearer
  Every day thy place of Rest,
Let then every step be clearer
  Though the spirit be oppressed;
    Ere long shall all thy fears be hushed,
    Ere long shall all thy foes be crushed,
      And thou wilt be at Rest.

Surer, weary Traveller, surer
  Step by step thy promised Rest,
Press to regions brighter, purer,
  None but these supremely blest;
    So great the blessing Jesus gives,
    His weary Saints Himself receives
      To His Eternal Rest.

LXXXVIII.

"This one thing I do, forgetting those things which are behind, and reaching forth unto those things which are before, I press toward the mark for the prize of the high calling of God in Christ Jesus." (Phil. iii. 13, 14.)

LORD, can I e'er Thy wondrous Love forget?
The joys unnumbered in my pathway set?
Each chastisement so lovingly applied,
No prayer unanswered, nor a good denied?
If Mercies past can e'er forgotten be
'Tis from some later one's intensity.

Yea, and I forward press, dear Lord, for this,
As chief ingredient in my cup of bliss;
For ever to be finding Love increase,
And fervent gratitude of Heart progress;
A clearer view of Mercy day by day,
Its knowledge reaching through Eternity.

Lord, can I e'er my Sin's career forget,
Still less the follies that encompass yet?
The sense of shame can ne'er be cast aside,
And nearer Home the less can follies hide;
But e'en as Sun is dazzling by its light,
So lost is thought of sin at Jesus' sight.

'Tis thus I press for glories yet beyond,
Love in the past of future love the bond;
Nay, I am called to higher things to rise,
The voice of Jesus tells me of my prize;
Mark for my soul, my heart's unerring aim,
By love encouraged Glory's Home I claim.

Prize worthy of the Giver, gift of love,
Can tongue e'er cease with Jesus' praise to move?
One thing I'll ne'er forget, to praise His Name,
And to Eternity His Love proclaim;
This privilege I learn yet more and more,
The nearer pressing to the Heavenly Shore.

CPSIA information can be obtained
at www.ICGtesting.com
Printed in the USA
LVHW100447110522
718424LV00003B/272

9 783375 003517